A Forbidden Love for Fire: The Power of a Dragon

Margaret A. Dyer

A Forbidden Love for Fire: The Power of a Dragon

Olympia Publishers
London

www.olympiapublishers.com
OLYMPIA PAPERBACK EDITION

Copyright © Margaret A. Dyer 2023

The right of Margaret A. Dyer to be identified as author of
this work has been asserted in accordance with sections 77 and 78 of
the Copyright, Designs and Patents Act 1988.

All Rights Reserved

No reproduction, copy or transmission of this publication
may be made without written permission.
No paragraph of this publication may be reproduced,
copied or transmitted save with the written permission of the publisher,
or in accordance with the provisions
of the Copyright Act 1956 (as amended).

Any person who commits any unauthorised act in relation to
this publication may be liable to criminal
prosecution and civil claims for damage.

A CIP catalogue record for this title is
available from the British Library.

ISBN: 978-1-80439-018-4

This is a work of fiction.
Names, characters, places and incidents originate from the writer's
imagination. Any resemblance to actual persons, living or dead, is
purely coincidental.

First Published in 2023

Olympia Publishers
Tallis House
2 Tallis Street
London
EC4Y 0AB

Printed in Great Britain

Dedication

Dedicated to all the strong men and women in my life

Daniel

There she stands, the new general of the Great British water nation. She is actually quite attractive; she has the most beautiful lily-white skin and luxurious long brown hair which she has curled with small plaits going round the crown of her head. As I examine her hair a little closer, I can see a small water nation pin tucked in the middle of the plaits – how cute.

She turns around to look at the crowd and I am immediately drawn to her eyes. I have never seen eyes so beautiful in all my life, so big and brown I could easily look into those eyes for the rest of my life. She has the most beautifully shaped body; she is a curvy girl. She is definitely the most beautiful woman I have seen so far in my life.

She is not only a beautiful woman but a woman that has made history: she is the very first female general of the water nation and to be honest probably the last. I look around the room where generals and soldiers from all four nations are stood. Not many are cheering; a fair few generals are against the idea of a woman becoming general.

She walks down towards Ivan the Russian water nation general and wraps her arms around him. She already looks overwhelmed and I can't say I blame her; I still remember the day I was crowned the fire nation general. Don't get me wrong, I was honoured, but I hated every minute of it.

My job is to look after and protect the people of the British fire nation as well as keep the peace with the other three nations.

I have only been general for four months and it is already challenging. Thankfully I have my best friend Jay by my side to help, if not I think I would jump off a cliff.

Jay is a very unique individual. He can be a bit on the crazy side sometimes but I can't complain; he is basically like my brother.

"Oi!" Speaking of the devil...

As much as I want to talk, I can't take my eyes off the new general.

"Excuse me?" Jay appears in front of me.

He is a tall, skinny guy with dirty blonde hair and fair skin, and he always has a straight face, unless he's drunk. He blocks my vision but it doesn't stop me thinking about her. I am suddenly met with a slap round the face and my attention is now set on Jay.

"Earth to Daniel, or do I need to give you another slap?"

I literally look at him in complete shock. "You are the only person in all four nations that can get away with shit like that."

He gives me the biggest grin known to man. "Oh please, I'm not the only one. Besides, it's worth it."

I dart my attention back to her; she is currently speaking to the Italian general. He's not a bad guy but can be a bit intense sometimes.

Jay lets out a slight laugh and takes a seat at the nearest table. I sit opposite him. He stares at me and continues to grin. "You fancy her?"

I smile and shake my head; he always has that on his mind. "I'm just examining her as we will now be working together closely."

He grins and starts to grab a load of food from the table "How close we talking?"

I roll my eyes and shake my head as he smiles at me. "Not too close, I hope."

I look up to see Valdameir, the fire nation general of Russia. He's a rather tall muscular man with short grey hair with little strands of white, bright green eyes and the warmest smile you could come across. I have all the time in the world for this man. He has been by my side through thick and thin and taught me how to be a man and saved me and Jay from a pretty shit situation. I give him a little smile.

"You know the rules, Daniel."

I let out a small laugh. "Yes, my lord, I know the rules."

He sighs and shakes his head. "How many times do I have to tell you, Daniel? Please call me Valdameir."

I smile at him. To be fair, he has told me to do that on more than one occasion. "Sorry, I forgot."

He laughs at me.

"He can at least offer her a dance, surely?" Jay asks him.

He gives me a look and rolls his eyes. "Fine, but nothing more, promise me."

I smile at him and nod. Jay and I get up and make our way over to the other side of the room to meet her. I don't know why but I grow increasingly nervous. I turn to Jay as I freeze on the spot. "Jay, I can't."

Jay stares at me and smiles. He looks me dead in the eyes. "Yes, you can, don't you dare pussy out on me, Daniel!"

I sigh and shake my head. "Jay, I can't dance."

He laughs at me. "Look around you. Most of the people in this room can't dance. You're not the only one."

I fix myself up a bit, and he rolls his eyes. We continue walking over. As we approach her I become even more nervous. If I thought she was beautiful before, I was absolutely correct;

she looks stunnin. She has a beautiful blue gown on with sapphires going across her chest. It is slim fitting which shows her figure perfectly.

"My lady." I bow, as does Jay. I take her hand and give it a little peck. Her big brown eyes gaze into mine, making me melt slightly.

"My lord." She smiles I have never seen a smile so beautiful.

"Congratulations, my lady, on becoming general. You must be proud." I smile at her but her smile quickly fades.

"Thank you, my lord. Yes, I am proud, I guess." I can tell by the look on her face that she is overwhelmed.

"My name is Daniel. I am the general of the fire nation and this is Jay, my co-general."

Her smile is back on her face. "Pleasure to meet you both. My name is Gemma and this is my co-general Frank."

He bows. "My lord." He is an older fella with brown hair with a few grey hairs, blue eyes and quite a muscular figure.

I look back at Gemma. "My lady, would you honour me with a dance?"

She smiles at me and looks at Frank. "Of course, my lord." She takes my hand and we make our way onto the dance floor.

Gemma

I stand there staring out the window looking down at the gardens out the front of the water nation house watching water nation generals from all over the world arrive. I watch as the Italian general gets out of his car and shake hands with the French general. I look around the gardens and the soldiers are helping the maids put out food and drink. Decorations are being placed around the gardens, not that they need it; the garden is beautiful and very well looked after, the grass a very healthy green with blossom trees and bushes covered in roses of all colours, my favourite being the white ones; they are unique just like me.

    I arrived at the water nation house yesterday morning. The current general showed me to my room, which is massive, by the way; on the left side of the room there is a huge fire place and in front there is a table and two chairs, all hand-made by a water nation soldier, I was told – he has quite the talent. To the right is my dressing table with all my makeup and hair equipment with a small mirror attached to it. If you walked further you would find the bathroom which is probably the biggest bathroom I have ever seen. It has a walk-in shower with a square head and clear glass, a big square mirror on the left wall and a pretty standard toilet and sink. On the back of the bathroom door is a bath robe and a towel. Next to the bathroom is a walk-in wardrobe which is filled with posh clothing which was pre-made for when I arrived, but my favourite part of the room is the bed, super king size, super cozy mattress with duck feather pillows and duvet. I do love my sleep. I collapse on my bed and curl up into a little ball. I start to dose off slightly until I hear my doors fly open.

"Some things never change, I see."

I look at the end of the bed to see Ivan, the water nation general of Russia. He quite small for a general, doesn't have much muscle, but he is very swift and talented. He has long, shoulder-length white hair, with bright blue eyes. He's not my father but he showed me how to manipulate my power of water, and he taught me the water nation's history, which is pretty boring, by the way. Behind him is Valdameir the fire nation general. He is the man of the hour. Valdameir is basically like my father, only he isn't. I am a very fortunate girl to have both of them in my life. Valdameir is also married, so his wife taught me how to be a lady, not that I am – I am basically more of a man than most men.

"Go away!" I bury my face in my pillow and cover my head with my duvet.

"Now, now, you need to get up. Today is the big day!" Ivan is so excited to watch me become general.

"I can't, Ivan. I'm not general material and I'm a woman – no one wants a woman as their general." For some reason all four nations have a thing about women not being generals. I will be the first ever female general in the history of the four nations.

"Don't be stupid. Yes, you can! The fire nation general was only crowned four months ago so you can learn together." Valdameir's face drops. "But don't get too close, of course." He smiles.

"Why would I get that close to a fire manipulator?"

They both laugh.

"Where is our girl?" Valdameir's wife Galina walks in and smile. She's a beautiful woman and looks quite young for her age. She has long blonde hair, hiding a few greys (which I'm sure were caused by me), a slim like figure, beautiful blue eyes and lily-white skin just like me.

"Some things never change."

In follows a dress. It is beautiful. I get out of my bed and walk towards the dress. It is dark blue with sapphire beading going across the chest area and very sliming.

"Boys, get out. Gemma needs to shower then change. Come back in two hours."

They both laugh and head out the door, leaving just me and Galina. "Shower now!"

After I take a nice hot shower I sit at my dressing table and let Galina blow-dry my hair. "You never know, you might find a man today to go with your general's title." She smiles. I stay quiet; I can't imagine anything worse right now. She heats up the curling tongs and starts to curl my hair. "I know you didn't want this, darling, but remember things happen for a reason and I know you of all people deserve this."

I look at her and smile. "Doesn't make it any better."

I turn round for her to put on a bit of makeup. She knows I like my makeup natural. "I don't want to find a man tonight anyway; I don't want a boyfriend."

She laughs at me. "These things happen unexpectedly, darling." I picked up my not-so-settle earrings; they are huge white diamonds on the outside and a sapphire in the middle. The necklace isn't any better, pretty much identical to the earrings only it is a necklace. "Come on, time for the dress." She makes it out to be like my wedding day but I am looking forward to putting on my dress. I slip into my dress and look into the mirror. It was a perfect fit, very slimming.

I turn to look at her. "So how do I look?"

She smiles. "Like a queen."

There is a knock at the door. "Are we allowed in yet?"

We both laugh. "Come in."

Ivan and Valdameir come through the door and look at me with massive grins on their faces. "You look absolutely stunning, darling." Ivan embraces me.

"It feels weird seeing our warrior princess like this but you do look beautiful." Valdameir gives me a massive hug. "We must get going as I have to join the fire nation. Good luck, my dear." He takes Galina's hand. "Come, my love–" they are so adorable "–it is time."

I all of a sudden feel really faint. I take Ivan's arm and walk out the room. Unfortunately, I am wearing heels. Me and heels are not friends. Just walking to the hall I nearly break my ankles.

We stop at these giant wooden doors. Ivan turns to face me. "Good luck."

He goes in and I imagine stands with the other water nation generals. I wish he was here just so I could hold on to him. I was already dead nervous, all I want to do is run away and bury my head in the sand as they say.

The doors open and I look into the room. It is huge. Not as big as the Russian one but still big. It has the water nation symbol plastered on every corner of the hall as well as the British flag hanging down the sides.

On my left is the air nation, down to earth people who don't really do or say anything. Next to them is the water nation; we are quite calm and accepting people but not in this situation. To my right is the earth nation. They aren't the nicest of people and as I was walk down I get some very deadly looks from them. Next to them is the fire nation, again not the nicest of people but some of them are decent like Valdamier and Galina.

I approach some steps and slowly make my way up them. In front of me are the water nation elders. They are the big bosses of the water nation; they say they are the voice of the ocean spirt, but I highly doubt it. A tall man with short brown hair, icy blue eyes and a chunky-like figure looks me square in the eyes. He wears a blue tux with a water nation pin.

"Good afternoon, everyone." I hear him start his speech and I start to zone out slightly. "Gemma?" Oh god the elder is talking to me now.

"Sorry, Elder Jeffery."

He looks at me, concerned. "Do you, Gemma, agree to look after the members of the Great British water nation, to put your life on the line for them and lead them into greatness?"

I take a deep breath. "I do."

He smiles. "Do you promise to keep the peace with the other nations and respect their ways?"

I look up at him. "I do."

He smiles at me again. "Will you work with the water nation elders to keep the water nation in order?"

I give him a little smile. "I will."

A soldier of the elders' army walks over with a cushion with a beautifully made crown on it, small, starling sliver I would say, with small sapphire diamonds. It really is beautiful. He places it on my head. He looks at me with his icy blue eyes and smiles. "Congratulations, my lady."

I turn around and face the crowd.

"Introducing the very first lady of the Great British water nation."

Many cheer, but most don't.

"Thank you all for coming to help me celebrate this historical day." I take a deep breath and look at Ivan. "I am looking forward to working with all of you to help guide the four nations into a brighter future, more importantly to me the water nation." I look down at a very close friend of mine that I have known for years, a lot older than me but I had to bring someone with me from Russia. "My co-general will be Frank Long, a very close friend of mine. I'm sure with his help and guidance I can be the general you all hope for me to be."

I walk down the stairs and make a beeline for Ivan. I pretty much fall into his arms. I honestly can't wait for this day to be over.

"Congratulations, I am so proud of you." I pull away from him and look him in the eyes. I could cry, to be honest.

"Congratulations!" Valdameir and Galina come over and both give me a massive hug.

"Thank you." I smile.

"Our warrior princess is now officially a queen."

I smile. Valdameir has always called me a warrior princess because I am stronger than most of his army, maybe even all of them.

I turn round and the Italian general Antonio approaches me. "Congratulations, my lady. I would like to introduce you to my son, Leonardo." Oh dear god here we go.

"Nice to meet you." I smile.

"I bet your heart is as beautiful as your eyes." That is the cheesiest thing I have ever heard in my life.

"Um, thank you." I look at Ivan who has a massive grin on his face. He is obviously finding this hilarious; I am having generals introducing me to their sons left right and centre.

"My lady." I turn round to see the most handsome man I have ever seen. He has short light brown hair, brown eyes, a slim like figure with a little bit of muscle. The only down side is he is fire nation.

"My lord."

He bows along with a guy who I assume is his co-general. "Congratulations, my lady, on becoming general. You must be proud." He smiles at me.

He asked me if I was proud – well, no, not really. "Thank you, my lord. Yes, I am proud, I guess."

He smiles at me again. He has quite a cheeky looking smile. "My name is Daniel. I am the general of the fire nation and this is Jay, my co-general."

I smile at him. "Pleasure to meet you both. My name is Gemma and this is my co-general Frank."

He bows. "My lord." Daniel bows back.

"My lady, would you honour me with a dance?" He holds out his hand. I look at Frank.

"Of course, my lord." I take his hand and we make our way over to the dance floor. Daniel faces me then places his left hand around my waist and takes my left hand in his right. I slide my right hand up his arm then the music play and we start to dance. We dance to the beautiful sound of the harp; it sort of suits this situation as I am up close to him looking into his eyes. Everything feels that little bit easier. He has a soft touch but naturally a warm touch, something I could get used to but sadly can't due to the difference in nations. I feel something a little weird about him though. He seems weirdly powerful, more powerful than Valdameir anyway.

"So, my lady, tell me more about yourself."

I smile at him. "What do you want to know?"

He pulls me in slightly closer. "Where are you from?"

I frown at him. "To be perfectly honest, I don't know. I was raised by Ivan and Valdameir, the Russian generals."

He looks at me, saddened. "Oh, well Ivan is a pretty good role model for anyone."

I smile at him. "What about you?"

He twists me around and brings me back into his arms. I don't want this dance to end but I can feel Valdameir watching us. Both of his hands are around my waist now. I wrap my arms around his neck. I going to be forever single, I think, because this is the only thing I could get used too.

"I'm from a town called Whitefall. I was found by the British general after I was kicked out."

Oh god, that's not good. Why would someone kick someone as good looking as him out? What did he do?

"Oh, why were you kicked out?"

He laughs. "Story for another day."

I smile at him. "That's a shame; I'm interested."

Okay, I am being a bit on the flirtatious side but I can't help it.

"My life isn't that interesting, my lady, trust me." He twists me around again then takes me back into his arms. "Can I just say, my lady, you look very beautiful tonight."

I smile and laugh a little. "Thank you, my lord. You don't look to bad yourself."

He laughs. He grips my hip slightly and pulls me in slightly closer so that our bodies are touching. I can feel everything. I look at Valdameir. He doesn't look best impressed with how close we re getting. "We are being watched."

He laughs again. "I know, Valdameir can be like that. But you were raised in Russia, so you know that."

I smile at him. "Oh, please, the amount of rules I broke while I was in Russia – he should know better by now."

He gives me a little laugh. "Then you have more balls than

me."

I actually enjoy his company. "Thank you from pulling me away from the crowd." I rest my head on his shoulder

"You're welcome, my lady." He rests his head on mine.

The music stops. We pull apart and bow to each other. "I will see you tomorrow then, my lady."

I smile at him. "Indeed. Good night, my lord."

I walk back over to the other generals to face the thunder once more.

Jay

Watching Daniel dance with Gemma is beautiful to watch. To be perfectly honest, I am a bit jealous. Daniel and I have known each other for eighteen years; we were raised by the previous fire nation general, unfortunately. We basically became brothers. I always have his back and he always has mine. He could have picked a better co-general but he needed someone he trusted and that is hard to find these days.

"My lord." The Russian co-general Mikhail approaches me.

"Ah, my lord, long time no see." He is basically like me but older; he is a tall man with dark brown hair and green eyes with a rather muscular figure.

"How are you?"

I smile. "Yeah, I'm okay. Still alive – that's good enough!"

He laughs. "Well that's something. Valdameir will not be happy about this."

As he points at Daniel, I give him a cheeky grin. "It's only a dance. What harm could it do?"

He looks at me, concerned. "It's Valdameir. He is very overprotective of her; he will be relying on Daniel to protect her."

I give him a serious look. "Why so overprotective?" I feel like rough times are coming.

"Just trust me, Jay. Valdameir is not stupid; he knows that there is something about her which makes her important."

I look at him, confused. I know that Valdameir isn't stupid, very far from it. "She is just a normal everyday water manipulator. What could make her so important?"

He looks at Gemma as she dances with Daniel and sigh. "Her power. I have never known anything like it. Just keep an eye on her, Jay."

I look at Daniel as he bows to her and heads my way; he has a massive grin on his face.

"Have fun?"

He looks at me then grabs a drink. "Yeah, she's nice. She will make a good general."

I laugh. God, he actually thinks I am that much of a mug. "You definitely fancy her."

He laughs. "Yes, she is attractive but she's water nation. It's forbidden, you know that."

I let out a massive laugh and down a shot of tequila. "Admit it, you were finding it hard not to rip her dress off and fuck her right there."

He laughs at me and takes a sip of his drink. I knew my best friend; that was definitely on his mind and you could see it on his face the whole time he was dancing.

"Sounds like you certainly had that on your mind."

I laugh at him and grab another drink. "You know what they say – picture your audience naked."

He chokes on his drink. "Rather not, thank you."

I laugh.

"Apparently she was quite the rebel in Russia."

I look at him funny. "She's Russian?"

He laughs and shakes his head. "No, she is British from the sounds of it but she was raised by the Russians. She is like us, has no idea who she is or where she comes from."

I shrug. I guess it is nice to know that there is someone else out there who knows how we feel. "wWell, would you look at that. Destiny has brought us all together."

He laughs. "Like old times?"

I raise my glass. He raises his and cheers me.

"Like old times."

He downs his drink and we drink the night away just like we used to, just missing the shagging girls bit. We play a secret drinking game and have so much fun, although a bit too much fun.

"You can tell you two are young."

We turn round and see Valdameir.

"Oops." I lean on Daniel's shoulder.

"We should retire, Jay. No rest for the wicked." He downs his drink.

"Oh! One more drink."

Daniel isn't even remotely drunk. It's like he is immune to that shit; he has never been drunk.

"No, young man! It is your duty to make sure your general gets home safe and sound. It is a good job Daniel is strong enough to defend himself," Valdameir literally snaps at me. I can't think of a single general that isn't shit scared of Valdameir. He definitely has that reputation.

"Yes, boss." Daniel was grinning at me the whole time.

"Let's go."

We walk back to the fire nation house as it is literally right next door and I stumble through the door. I make my way to my room and pass out onto my bed.

Valdameir

Watching the beautiful young girl I raised become general made me so proud. She was always such a strong soul – kicked my ass on more than one occasion.

"Valdameir." I turn to see her beautiful smile glaring at me.

"Gemma." She embeds herself in my arms just like she used to when she was a little girl. I stroke the back of her head and kiss her on her forehead. "Are you okay, my dear?"

She looks up at me and rests her chin on my chest. "I'm going to miss you and Galina. I don't want you to go."

I smile. I cup her cheek and pull away slightly. "And we will miss you, but you know that if there are any issues we will always be a phone call away." She gives me that beautiful smile but I notice she seems a bit down. "What is it, dear?"

She sighs and shakes her head. "It's nothing, just nervous, you know."

I give her a little laugh. "I'm not silly, Gemma." I take her hands in mine.

"You know when I had that dance with the fire nation general?" I nod with a little bit of rage going through me. "I felt a ridiculous amount of power go through him. It was weird."

I didn't think she was at that stage yet. I rub my chin then smile. "I will look into it but I do not want you to worry. Just do your job in keeping the water nation safe." I kiss her on the forehead.

The Italian water nation general is walking over with his son who is around the same age as Gemma, maybe a few years older, and yes, he is attractive but Gemma clearly isn't interested and he has been bothering her all night. She even went through the pain of a dance.

"Valdameir, please help me get rid of him; he keeps trying to hook me up with his son."

I laugh a little as the Italian water nation general approaches.

"My lord, my lady." I give him a small bow and Gemma gives him a small smile. "Valdameir, I hear you raised this beautiful new general. May I ask how, seen as you are fire nation?"

Gemma gives me a look begging me to get rid of him.

"Well, I had Ivan's help when it came to the water manipulation bit but I did the rest; I taught her how to lead, how to fight and raised her."

Gemma gives him another small smile.

"I see. Well, I think we can all agree that she surely won't be able to do this on her own. I have been speaking with Ivan about a possible marriage between her and my son Leonardo."

Gemma crosses her arms, shakes her head and turns to me.

"And I am afraid that is not up to Ivan. He may have trained her to water manipulate but I raised her and the answer is no."

He looks at me, intrigued. "She's a woman, Valdameir; she can't possibly lead a nation."

I give him an evil grin. "Oh please, my lord, she could do a much better job than any man in this room. Leadership is in her blood, trust me."

He grins. "Maybe this will be the one time the well-respected Russian general Valdameir is wrong."

All I can do was smile, knowing I am right. "Gemma, my dear, why don't you head to bed. You look tired."

She smiles, gives me a hug and a kiss on the cheek, looks at the Italian general and his son, then goes off to find Galina.

Mikhail comes up behind me. "Everything okay here, Valdameir?"

I look at him and smile. "He seems to think he can marry his son to Gemma."

Mikhail laughs and taps me on the shoulder. "Good luck getting Valdameir's blessing. You will have to work a miracle to get that."

The Italian general smiles. "We got Ivan's."

I laugh, as did Mikhail. "Ivan has no idea what she is like. He wouldn't be able to handle her, trust me."

He laughs. "She's a woman, no different from the others."

I grin. "Oh, trust me, she is very different."

Mikhail hands me a piece of paper. I look down and my smile fades. I look back up to the Italian general. "If you do not mind, I have to now go and do my job."

I walk away from him and walk into one of the spare bedrooms with Mikhail and Galina. I read the note over and over again. "Where did you get this?"

Mikhail shrugs. "One of the soldiers gave it to me."

I think this is a bit on the odd side.

"What does it say, darling?"

I sigh. "All it says is that fire manipulators are being taken from local towns." Galina raises an eyebrow. "What of the soldier that gave this too you?"

Mikhail shrugs again. "After he gave it to me, he vanished out of thin air."

I strok my chin. I have to let Daniel know. I stroke Galina on the cheek, kiss her on her beautiful pink lips. "Come, dear, I have to speak with Daniel and you must get some rest for the journey tomorrow."

She wraps her arms around me. "Must we go so early? She hardly settled in."

I kiss her again and tuck her hair behind her ear. "We must. I have stuff to do back home. Do not worry, she will contact us if needed." I take her hand and we walk out to make our way to the fire nation house.

Daniel

The last few hours of the party were amazing, just like old times. We were laughing, drinking and just genuinely having fun. Jay always finds a way of getting that side out of me but unfortunately it was short lived as I have a job to do.

Jay can get as paralytic as he wants. Me, well, I can't exactly get drunk even if I wanted to. Jay and I arrived home and he passed out in his bedroom while I sat in front of the fire with another glass of rum. I can hardly sleep these days but I can't stop thinking about Gemma. Her beautiful brown eyes, her long brown hair, how it felt to have her up close to me, her smile – God, that smile is just beautiful – the feel of her hand making its way up my arm, her soft and smooth hand in mine and the urge to kiss her was strong but I couldn't but it is scary how similar we are.

I hear a knock at my door.

"Who is it?" It can't be Jay because hes probably passed out by now.

"It's the Russian general, my lord."

Another lecture, as if I haven't had enough from him already.

"Come in." If I don't let him in, he will just come in anyway.

"Daniel."

I lookat him and smile. "Valdameir." He sitin the chair on the other side of the table and pours himself a drink. "Towhat do I owe the pleasure?"

Valdameir smile. "Did you have fun tonight?"

I roll my eyes. "Not too much fun, I promise." I knew what

he was implying.

"I am relying on you, Daniel, to look out for her. Not many people agree with a woman being general."

I laugh and pour myself another drink. "Well you don't know if you don't try and from what I have learned about her already I am sure she will be just fine."

He laughs and takes a sip of his drink. "I hope you do not mind, Daniel, but me and Galina are staying in the room just a few doors down. I want her to get a good night's sleep before the journey home tomorrow."

I shrug and shake my head. "Valdameir, you know that you out of all people are allowed to stay in whatever room you please. Me and Jay wouldn't be here if it wasn't for you." I suddenly pause as I notice he is giving me a serious look. "What?" He looks me dead in the eyes then looked down, saddened. "Is it Galina? Is she okay?"

He shakes his head. "Daniel, I have received word of fire manipulators going missing in local towns."

I give him a glare then a sudden surge of rage comes over me and I throw the glass I have in my hand to the other side of the room and watch it smash into millions of little pieces.

"Daniel, calm down."

For some reason I can't control it; I can feel myself heating up. "Typical! I sit here drinking and partying while innocent fire manipulators are being taken from their families." I pick up the chair and smash it against the wall next to me, causing the chair to break. "Some general I am."

Valdameir stands up and looks at me, shocked, as if he has never seen anything like it. "Daniel, you need to remain calm. None of this is your fault. You can't do anything about it if you don't know about it, can you?"

He has a point. I collapse on my bed and cover my face with

my hands. Valdameir sits on the bed next to me.

"Daniel, you're a good general, but you have only been general for four months. You're being too hard on yourself."

I look up at him. "What am I meant to do, Valdameir?"

He smiles. "All you can do is find out exactly who these people are and where they have been taken to and bring them back to their families."

I look back up to the ceiling. "I know exactly who did this, Valdameir." He looks at me, confused. "The most dangerous fire manipulator I know." I look back at him. "Dan Val Gule." I sit up and look at the dragon figure carved into my wall. "I have to find him."

Valdameir looks at me in shock. "Daniel, you are jumping to conclusions."

Why is he backing this traitor up? The elders have been hunting this man down for years and Valdameir wants me to scrap the only reason for me to find him?

"I'm convinced, Valdameir. He has to be behind it."

Valdameir looks at me, concerned. "Very well, Daniel, but don't just focus on him Remember there are others out there that could have done this."

I know who he means and that look; he is not convinced that Dan Val Gule has anything to do with it. "I know. I guess I'm just trying to drown him out but being general its difficult. I see his name everywhere."

Valdameir walks up to me and taps me on the shoulder. "I know, Daniel, but it is okay. Someday he will get what is coming to him." I give him a small smile. "Good night, Daniel."
I nod at him and watch him walk out the room. I sit on my bed for a while before I put my uniform back on and make my way to my office. I will find Dan Val Gule and I will get answers.

Gemma

Finally, the evening is over. I slowly walk back to my room as my feet are killing me from wearing these horrible heels all night. It honestly feels like someone has been scrubbing the bottom of my feet with a cheese grater.

All the generals certainly have mixed opinions on me becoming general, which is why I was constantly being introduced to their sons. It was driving me fucking nuts, which is one of the reasons I went over to Valdameir before bed.

I needed to get away although I can't stop thinking about my dance with Daniel, the way it felt to be close to him, his chest on mine, his hand slowly making its way around my waist, nice and warm,

I lean against the wooden doors visualising it in my head. It is actually turning me on slightly. I loved every minute of that dance. I undress myself thinking about how much I want to see him again, thinking of those eyes, those brown eyes looking down at me. I replay it over and over again in my head. I know he's a fire manipulator but a girl can only dream, right?

I start to think about what he looks like underneath his uniform. I am definitely going to be single for life.

I go into my wardrobe and open one of the draws where all of my night gowns are. I look through them and find a small light pink satin night gown with black stitching going across the top and the bottom. I look up in front of me and see a long, black, sort of see-through dressing gown with feathered edges. I take them both and get myself ready for bed. I put on my night gown and look at myself in the mirror. It makes me look very sexy, shapes my body perfectly, gives me a lot of cleavage and shows off the bottom of my bum. It makes me feel very good.

I place on my dressing gown and walk over to my dressing table. I sit in front of the mirror and start to remove my makeup. I pick up my brush and brush my hair through until I am convinced most of the hairspray is out and my hair feels that little bit soft again. I remove all my jewellery and place it all carefully in their boxes. I finally feel a little bit like me again.

I stare at myself in the mirror for a while then make my way over to my bed. I hang up my dressing gown and sit up in my bed for a bit. I grab my book that I brought with me and start reading. I can't go to sleep without reading; it my imagination going. My favourite is a good old forbidden love story – they are the best kind.

I get through a fair bit of my book then I start to feel tired. I put my book down and turn off the lamp. I curl up into a little ball then start to dose off.

I hear a knock at my door.

"Who is it?" I am sure this will happen quite a lot so I'd best get used to this.

"It's Frank, my lady."

It's only Frank so it's not that bad. "Come in."

Frank opens the door and strolls in. I turn my lamp on and he stands at the end of my bed. "My apologies, my lady, I didn't mean to disturb you this late."

I smile at him. "It's okay. And please call me Gemma; you're my co-general."

He gives a little laugh. "The fire nation general has asked to speak with us tomorrow about something urgent." Oh, what could he want that could possibly be this urgent? "As it will be your first day as general, I can turn round and say no."

I smile at him. I know he is only thinking about me. "No, it's okay, it is urgent so we'd best not keep him."

Frank smiles and nods. "Very well, tomorrow we shall enter the dragon's den." I laugh. "Good night, my lady." Frank has always been the formal type so I don't think that will ever change.

"Good night, Frank." I smile.

He walks out the room. I lay back down in my bed. What could he possibly want to talk to me about? Is it about our dance? I think about the love stories I have read and about what the characters would do in my situation. I hope it won't be awkward between us but now that has occurred, I can't take him off my mind. Those eyes, his touch, the feel of his muscles...

My hands start to slowly move down. I remove my knickers and continue to think about Daniel, about what it would feel like to feel him inside me. I place my fingers inside myself and start to moan a little. It's not every day I get to dance with a hot guy. I imagine every detail from every inch of his face to the feel of his arms to the feel of his touch. I start to get a little loud so I quieten down a little. I grip the pillow next to me as I orgasm. I feel a sense of relief. I get up wash myself up, get back into bed and slowly drift off to sleep.

Frank

Being asked millions of questions about how I plan on running the water nation feels cruel; I know that Gemma will make a fabulous general. Sure it will be difficult and there will be things that test her but she has been raised by the best. However, I saw her dance with that young general – Daniel I think his name is – and I became concerned. I have seen that look before, the look they gave each other. I know she is rather beautiful and can distract any man from their job but I now feel like my role as co-general is going to be tested.

I hear a knock at my door.

"Who is it?" There is a short pause. I open the door and see Dean, the captain of the army.

"Pardon me, my lord, but the fire nation captain gave me this to give to the general but I didn't want to disturb her."

I nod. "Thank you, Dean."

He bows and walks off. I look down at the letter:

Dear Gemma,
I was wondering if you could come by the fire nation house at nine a.m. tomorrow morning. I require your help with a problem that I have and would also like to make you aware of it.
Again, congratulations on making history.
Daniel
Fire Nation General of Great Britain

What problem is he talking about and why is he asking a new fresh general to help him with this particular issue? Thankfully I am fully clothed so I walk towards Gemma's room and knock on the door.

"Who is it?"

I take a small sigh. "It's Frank, my lady."

Gemma has four guards outside her door, probably Valdameir's doing. "Come in."

I walk in as she turns her lamp on and sits up in her bed. "My apologies, my lady, I didn't mean to disturb you this late."

She smiles at me. "It's okay. And please call me Gemma; you're my co-general." I give her a little laugh. She is so sweet and kind but she does also know that I am more of a formal guy.

"The fire nation general has asked to speak with us tomorrow about something urgent." She looks at me, confused and concerned at the same time. "As it will be your first day as general, I can turn round and say no." I am only thinking of her; I don't want her to overdo it.

"No, it's okay, it is urgent so we'd best not keep him." I know she is secretly dreading it after their dance.

I smile at her. "Very well, tomorrow we shall enter the dragon's den." She laughs at me. "Good night, my lady." Now she has a title I want her to get used to it.

"Good night, Frank."

I smile, turn and make my way out of her room. I close the door and look at the guard. "Guard that door with your life."

He nods. "I have no intentions of leaving it, my lord."

I smile at him. "Training, seven a.m. tomorrow." They all nod and one goes to spread the word. I make my way back to my room thinking about what the issue could possibly be.

Jay

"Jay."

I hear a voice in my head although I can't make it out.

"Jay."

I place my pillow over my head trying to make the voice go away. "Fuck off, I want to sleep."

I am suddenly hit with the feeling of ice-cold water being thrown all over me. "Fuck my life!"

I leap out of bed soaking wet, ready to attack, but look in front of me and see Daniel holding an empty steel bucket.

"You should know better than to wake up a man when he is sleeping, especially a man with a hangover."

He gives me the most evil grin I have seen. It is not the first time he has done this, to be fair; I know how much he enjoys this. He might be my best friend but right now I could easily kill him.

"You know how much I enjoy waking you up after a party."

I am fucking freezing and before I know it Daniel is being given another bucket of water. He throws it all over me once again and gives me another grin. "I wasn't satisfied that you where awake enough."

I give him a deadly look. "Fuck you, Daniel."

He laughs. "My office, ten minutes, no later."

Ten minutes, my ass. I will take as long as I want. I take a shower and put on a fresh set of uniform. My head hurts and I am so tired I could easily collapse on my bed and go back to sleep, but I walk down the hall to Daniel's office and see him looking through a few papers. I collapse on the chair opposite him.

"Thirty minutes? I said ten."

I look at him and have so much hate for him right now I could kill him. I look up at the clock and notice the time. "Daniel it's six in the morning. What could possibly be so important that I need to be awake at six in the morning?" I literally have no energy for this shit. I just want to go back to bed. I look over at Daniel who is literally staring at me with the most serious look known to man. It has just occurred to me that Daniel might have pulled an all-nighter. "What is it?"

He looks me square in the eyes. He looks absolutely shattered; you can see the bags under his eyes. "Fire manipulators have been taken from our local towns."

Well that's not good. "Oh dear, that's not good."

He slams a book down onto the table and stands up. "NO, JAY, ITS NOT!"

Jesus Christ, I don't think I have ever seen Daniel this angry. "Daniel, calm down. We will sort it."

He walks over to the window and looks back at me. "How, Jay, how am I supposed to sort it when I don't even know where to start?"

Oh dear god. "What do you mean?"

He leans against the window and starts to burn the window ledge with his hands. "Daniel, I mean it – calm down. You can start with thinking about a few people that it could be."

He picks up a load of stuff and starts throwing it about. At this point I'm scared of him and I have never been scared of him.

"There is only one man I can think of that could possibly do something like this." He is now setting things on fire which is not good.

"Daniel, we can start there. Let's see if there are any

connections between his crimes and the missing fire manipulators. There might be some sort of connection."

He calms down slightly. "Jay, why am I general? I am meant to protect these people and I can't even do that."

I take the plunge and walk over to him. "Daniel, you have only been general for four months, no one expects you to get things right all the time. Come on, let's get started." I lead Daniel over to his desk and he starts to look through some of the papers of the missing people and I look at the papers of his previous crimes. Something is wrong with him; I have never seen him like this and for some reason he has become more powerful and more angry. It worries me.

Fire Nation Soldier 1

I stand outside listening to the general's conversation with our co-general and I grow a little concerned about his ability to lead. I know he is young and he has been through hell but maybe for once the Russian general was wrong.

I start hearing things being thrown about and smell burning coming from inside the room which means he is angry. The previous general hadn't been any better; in fact, he had been a lot worse and hadn't got on with a lot of people. I am loyal to him and always will be but I am worried he has made so many mistakes already and although this new general is rumoured to be quite beautiful I am worried she will become a distraction.

I hear a load of whispers coming from the great hall so I walk away from the office and peek my head around to see what s going on. I see a load of soldiers in a little group and start to listen very carefully.

"He's weak. He should never have become general." I wouldn't say he is weak exactly; he's just young and he hasn't been general for that long.

"The previous general should have just let him die." Bit harsh, but to be honest it would have done Daniel a favour. The previous general put Daniel through hell.

However, they are bad mouthing our general and I don't know what to do. I am taken away from my thoughts as the doors fly open and in comes her ladyship. She looks like she means business. She is basically wearing battle gear but I suppose because she s new and a female she is being wary of what the people around her are doing. You could see the water nation soldiers looking round the room assessing every soldier in the room. At least they are loyal but that is the nature of the water nation.

No one approaches her so I take the plunge. "Good morning, my lady, how are you?"

She smiles at me as two soldiers step forwards slightly. "Good morning. I am very good, thank you. How are you?"

She seems quite sweet to be fair.

"I'm very good, thank you. To what do we owe the pleasure?"

She smiles at me again. "Good. Your general requested to see me."

Out of all people but I can see why it does seem like she means business. I lead her to the general's office and knock on the door. "My lord?"

There is a small silence.

"Who is it?" He sounds tired and stressed.

"The lady of the water nation has arrived." I look at her and smiles.

"Let her in." I open the door and let her in. The general looks at me. "Thank you." He nods. Hopefully he is able to concentrate otherwise this could be a problem.

Gemma

My first day as the water nation general has officially started and I am dreading it. My mind is still all over the place and I am still thinking about my dance with Daniel; I shouldn't be but it seems to be the only thing keeping me going. I lie in my bed thinking about what it would feel like being in his arms again, to feel his warm body up against mine. I smile at the thought of it. Unfortunately, I have to face him today and make sure I stay professional. Besides, I have a job to do.

I manage to gain the strength to get out of bed. I was never one for early mornings. I look out the window and see my army at training. The water nation training program is nowhere near as hard as the fire nation's; Valdameir made me do theirs just so I could be that little bit stronger than everyone else. Every time, I was wiped out for the rest of the day. Valdameir found it funny of course but it made me their warrior princess.

I make my way over to the bathroom to take a shower. I stand there in the shower thinking about him. I decide to quickly wash my hair and my body and make my way to my wardrobe. I look for something to wear and literally can't find anything. These people don't know me at all; they are all dresses and skirts, some formal and some professional. Finally, I spot a very detailed top – it looks like a two-in-one but stitched together. It has a sweetheart neckline which will definitely show cleavage and it look rather tight. Next to it is some slim like trousers. It s my first day as general, I may as well make myself feel good. On my way out I spot some armor, I assume for battle, steel waist with a point which I assume goes between the breasts and a set of steel arm guards with the water nation symbol on them. Why not – you never know what's round the corner.

I get myself dressed then look at myself in the mirror. Damn, I look good! My cleavage is massively on show which is something I have never been able to help but it makes me feel good, in a way. At least I can start my first day as general with a blast.

I dry my hair and make sure it is set to my satisfaction, put on a little bit of mascara and make my way downstairs. I walk out to the training grounds and watch my army train. I request for a table and chairs to be brought out so I can watch. They bring my breakfast out to me which Valdameir probably had something to do with; egg and soldiers, my favourite. I have always loved it ever since I was a kid. He must have told the chef before he left.

Frank walks up the steps and sits in the chair opposite me. "My lady."

I nod. "Frank." He smiles; he knows I will forever call him that because he is a friend.

"Sleep well?" I nod. "Thought I would make sure the army got in a training session before we enter the dragon's den."

I laugh; he is not entirely wrong, to be fair. "I agree. Thank you." He smiles at me. "Make sure the army is fed and watered before we leave and pick out six soldiers to come with us." He looks at me, confused. "What?"

He sighs. "My lady, take at least ten."

Oh dear god, here we go. But he is only doing his job. "No, six will be fine. You need to remember who raised me." I smile.

He smiles in return, knowing that I have a valid point; anyone would be a fool to touch me. "On it, my lady." He gets up and goes to select six soldiers to come with us to, as he would call it, the dragon's den.

Daniel

After pulling an all-nighter looking into Dan Val Gule's previous crimes to see if any of this relates to my current problem, I have nothing. I don't even know where he is. He has literally gone off the radar; no one has seen him.

Jay has taken over on most of the work because I am so tired, I can't physically think anymore. This is the problem with my job.

"Are you one hundred percent sure it's him?"

I look at Ja. He already knows I'm in a bad mood – why would he ask me that question? "Yes, it has to be; he is the most wanted fire manipulator in the world, he has a reputation, and he is top of my list of people to find and kill."

Jay gives me a funny look. "That's a flat-out lie." I look at him, confused. "The previous general is – I'm pretty sure you hate him more than anyone else on this planet."

I mean, he's not wrong.

Jay looks down at a piece of paper and goes as white as a sheet.

"What?"

He gulps. "Daniel, what town did you say you were from again?" He looks at me, terrified.

"Whitefall. Why?"

He looks down at the piece of paper and back up to me. "He burnt down a village called Whitefall. No survivors." I look at Jay in complete shock. "Eighteen years ago."

I start to feel sick. That was the year I was kicked out. That was the year I lost everything all because I am who I am.

"Daniel, are you okay?"

I suddenly feel faint. If I had been there, I would have been roasted alive. There is a knock at the door, dragging me away from my thoughts.

"My lord." It is one of my soldiers.

"Who is it?" I do recognise the voice but I'm not too sure.

"The lady of the water nation has arrived."

I get up and fix myself up a bit. I look at Jay and he grins.

"Let her in."

My soldier opens the door and she walks through the door. Oh my god, you can see everything, every curve, cleavage, the lot. She looks absolutely amazing.

"My lord." She smiles, again that smile making me melt.

"My lady." I walk over to her and take her hand to give it a peck. "Welcome to the fire nation." I smile at her and stare at her dead in those big brown eyes while still holding her hand.

"Thank you, my lord."

I lead her over to the seat in front of my desk and pour her a glass of water. She nods to say thank you.

"So, first day, how's it going so far?" I smile at her but I can't take my eyes of her breasts; it's bad, really.

"It's okay. I haven't really had much to do, which is a good sign, I hope." She smiles at me and leans back in the chair.

I return the smile. "That is about to change, my lady, unfortunately. Have you heard of someone called Dan Val Gule?"

She looks at me concerned and her smile drops. "I have indeed; Valdameir has told me about him. Very interesting man. And please, call me Gemma."

I smile at her – I wasn't expecting first name terms already, to be honest. "Good, then we are on the same page. What has Valdameir told you about him? And please call me Daniel."

She takes a sip of water. "Just that he is an enemy of the fire nation with an interesting story."

Jay is giving me very dirty-minded looks; the sod definitely has sex on his mind and I'm not going to deny it, I am finding it a bit difficult to be professional at the moment.

"What about him?" Frank questions.

"We think he has been taking innocent fire manipulators from local towns." I hand Gemma the list of fire manipulators that are missing.

"I see. I am assuming you want my help finding these fire manipulators?"

I nod. "If you don't mind."

I smiled at her but she looks at me confused. "Why not someone more experienced like the earth nation general or the air nation general? Why me?"

I give her a small laugh. "Because the earth nation general is a prick and doesn't care about anyone else and the air nation like to stay out of drama which admittedly the fire nation usually does too. So you are his only option," Jay explains and he was one hundred percent correct. The earth nation general and I do not get on at all and the air nation would rather stay out of it.

"I see, and what makes you think I would help?" Beautiful and smart – I like it.

"Because you actually have a heart and you want to help return these fire manipulators back to their families just as much as I do." Jay looks at me in slight shock.

"Very well, if I did help you what is your master plan?"

I smile at her then look at Jay.

"OH, COME ON!" He knows exactly why I'm looking at

him.

"Wait, you're planning on using your co-general as bait, are you mad?"

I nod. "Jay is more than capable of fighting his way out as well as talking his way out." I wasn't wrong; Jay has a talent when it comes to talking. He can literally talk his way out of anything.

"Are you serious? He is meant to be by your side all the time and now you're risking his life!" She is bent over and lent up against the desk and I can see right down her top. This has now been made impossible; the problem is I am shit at flirting.

"Yes, he denies it but he loves it."

She looks at me, disgusted. "If you want to risk Jay's life, fine, but don't come running to me for help. I will help you find them, yes, because I have a heart, but I don't agree with how you're handling it." I stand up and come level with her, although she is shorter than me. I walk up close to her. "If something happens to Jay, it's not on me."

I nod. "Very well, thank you for agreeing to help me find them."

She stares at me for a while. "I must go. Good day, Daniel."

I smile at her. "Good day, Gemma."

She is furious. She walks out the room with Frank and shuts the door behind her.

"Something tells me she disagrees. I have no idea what it is," Jay says sarcastically. I look at Jay knowing he is right. "You're not getting some anytime soon."

I roll my eyes and sit back at my desk. "You start tomorrow – eight till five in the nearest town. If you see anything suspicious or get the feeling something is about to happen, come straight back, do you understand?"

He makes an army salute. "YES, SIR!"

I laugh. "Jay, I am going to have to get some sleep. Do you mind taking over for a bit?"

Jay shakes his head. I get up from my desk and Jay takes a seat at my desk. I walk out the room and make my way to my room. I am so tired; my energy has run out. I really hope tomorrow goes to plan.

Jay

My alarm starts to go off and I throw it across the room. I bury my head in my pillow and moan. Seven in the morning.

Today is my first day going undercover. As excited as I am, I am also dreading every minute of it. I finally find the strength to get up and take a nice hot shower. I must spend about twenty-odd minutes in the shower just to wake up – I have never been one for early mornings and that will never change. I get out the shower and walk through my wardrobe to see what I can find that won't give me away as much. I find an old pair of light blue jeans, plain white top and a brown jacket. I didn't even know I had this stuff but I suppose it will do. I put on all my undercover clothes and begin to walk out the door when I am stopped by one of Daniel's soldiers.

"Good morning, my lord, how are you?"

I am so tired I can't even process much. "Good morning. I am very tired but okay, thank you."

He nods and smiles. "Good. My lord, may I speak with you quickly before you go?"

I raise an eyebrow, interested in what he has to say. "Of course?" Why is he not going straight to Daniel? "What's up?"

He looks at me, struggling to get the words out. "My lord, I didn't know what else to do. I didn't want to go to the general because I didn't know what he would stay?"

Hmm, he's obviously scared of Daniel which is good and bad at the same time. "Any reason you feel like you can't go to him?"

He looks down at the floor then looks back up to me. "My lord, I feel he can get quite angry pretty quickly lately and I do sometimes fear for my life."

Well that's not good, however Daniel has been pretty good at losing his temper lately and he is very difficult to control. "I understand that – I'm working on it. What did you want to tell me?"

He takes a deep breath. "My lord, I heard some soldiers speak ill of the general yesterday before her ladyship arrived."

Hmm, interesting. "What where they saying?" I can already tell by the glum look on his face that they were really not good.

"They said that the previous general should have left him to die and that he is weak."

Ha, after what I saw yesterday, he is anything but weak. "Okay, listen, everyone is allowed to have an opinion but he has only been general for four months. He is anything but weak and to be honest the previous general would have done him a favour if he'd left him to die." He looks at me, confused. "However, that man cares about every single one of you, will have all your backs whenever you need him, so those men need to stop looking at his mistakes and start looking at his achievements. He is twenty-two years old and he has been to hell and back already."

He looks at me and nods. "that is what I thought, my lord, which is why I came to you."

I cab understand that, with Daniel being the way he has been lately – I can't blame the poor man. "I understand that, but just know that he does care about you and the fire nation would be nothing without him; he is a lot stronger than you think you know." He nods again. "Just do me a favour and keep an eye on it. I want a full report when I get back. I will have a quick word with the water nation general before I go and above all, keep him alive."

He bows. "Of course, my lord. Thank you." I nod in approval and he walks out the room.

I am going to have to speak to Gemma. I know for a fact something isn't right. I make my way to the great hall and spot Daniel standing next to Gemma. I grin at him.

"Late as usual."

I laugh. "Well, what can I say? Pure perfection takes time." He laughs and gives me a bro hug. "Don't do anything stupid while I'm gone."

He lets go and looks at me funny. I smile, I walk over to Gemma as she opens her arms for a hug. I hug her in return. "Gemma, look after him. I feel like there is something going on with him but I can't put my finger on it."

She looks at me and smiles. "Of course I will."

I walk out the door and make my way to my car. It's not exactly posh; it's only a Ford Fiesta 2012 version, nothing special. I start the engine and make my way to the nearest town. The closest town with the most fire manipulators in it is Littleton, quite a small town. I have been there once or twice with Daniel back in the good old days – you know, when Daniel was fun – and of course to my luck it started pissing it down with rain. Classic Britain.

I park up outside a little cafe and decide to get a hot chocolate before I walk through the town centre. Despite the weather the market is still going. "APPLES, COME AND GET YOUR APPLES, FRESH AND JUICY." Yes, I admit it, my mind went straight in the gutter.

I walk through the Victorian-style village and look around for any signs of suspicious activity and so far I have nothing, I decide to stop at another cafe and grab a bite to eat. No one can beat a good old bacon sandwich. That's the thing about the fire nation – we are meat lovers and that will never change, which is why you can tell this village is dominated by fire nation. There are a fair few meat stools, fruit and veg stools, and stools selling little self-made bits. It's quite a nice little village to be fair; I could retire here easily.

I spot an antique shop across the road which I have never seen before and decide to go and take a look. I walk in and see all sorts of different little bits ranging from wooden tables and chairs, music boxes and small little window figures. One particular figure catches my eye: a small dragon painted red. The scales on it have a little bit of shine to them. It is sleeping on bright green grass. It isn't a small dragon, either; you can tell that if this particular dragon were life size, he would be huge. Daniel's birthday is coming up so I thought while I was here, I would buy him a little gift.

"Like dragons, do you?"

I jump out to my skin and turn to see an old man with scruffy white hair and small glasses, which he wears sitting just at the end of his nose. He looks at me just over the top of them, I am assuming they are for reading. He is wearing a white striped shirt which seems a bit too big for him and light brown trousers that come just above the ankles. He looks quite a lot like a grandad and I am sure he is.

"Love them. Me and my best friend have always wanted a dragon each." He smiles; he definitely has that warm grandad smile. "How much?" I walk over to the till and present him with the dragon figure.

"Six pound fifty."

I give him seven pounds. I have noticed that not many people come in here but I love it. "How long has this been here?"

He grins. "Years."

I look at him, confused. "Really? Me and my best friend used to come here all the time and we never saw it."

He laughs. "You seem young. I'm sure all you were focusing on were the pubs, and of course the girls."

I mean, he's not wrong.

"Have you ever seen a dragon?" Given his age, I was hoping he would say yes.

"Of course! They are even around in this day and age."

I laugh. "I wish! I would love just once to see a dragon."

He smiles at me. "They actually say that the dragon sprit himself walks this earth in human form." He looks down at my dragon.

I highly doubt it.

"Got any stories about them?"

He smiles at me again. "Course I do."

I stand there listening to all his stories and adventures he has had. As time is getting on decide it is time to leave. "Thank you for your time and all your stories but I must get off; time is getting on."

He nods. "Go careful out there. Strange things happen out in those streets."

Right, yeah. I nod at him and make my way out of the shop. I start walking down the street and put the dragon figure in the inside pocket of my coat. I freeze slightly as I notice there is no one about, not a single person; none of the stools are open nor are the cafes or shops. It is completely silent. I start to jog towards my car. I get to my car and notice the windows are broken and the tyres are slashed. Someone knows I'm here. I walk up the street slightly, using all my senses to figure out what's going on around me. I back track to what the soldier told me before I left and replay it in my head. "Some soldiers were speaking ill of our general." Something isn't right.

I suddenly hear footsteps coming up behind me.

"The co-general of the fire nation. You will certainly make a fine prize."

I clench my fists as they light up in flames. "You don't want to do this, buddy."

He laughs. I see another walking in front of me but I can't make out who it is.

"Oh, please. You're vulnerable; Daniel isn't here to help." I recognise the voice but I can't think where from.

Two come charging at me from the sides. My arms fly up either side. I unclench my fists and fire comes flying out of both of my palms forcing the attackers to defend themselves by trying to control the fire. Keeping my hands flat, I slowly move one hand above my head and another sliding across my stomach. I turn my body to my right, legs apart with my hands in the same position. I wait a few seconds and clench my fists, causing the fire to surround me. I turn my body back to face the attackers with my fists still clenched. I raise my arm up in front of me, ready to laugh the attack when I feel a small object pierce my shoulder. I look at my right shoulder and there is a small syringe with fluid inside it which is making its way into my body. I all of a sudden feel really faint and start to see double. Eventually I see nothing and pass out.

Daniel

17:05. Jay hasn't returned home.

I give it the benefit of the doubt and put it down to traffic. I stand by the window of my office waiting for his car to pull up but an hour later he still hasn't returned. Something isn't right. I know Jay can be late on the odd occasion but not this late and he would let me know if he was going to be this late. I walk out of my office and find a few soldiers. "Get the car ready. We're going to Littleton."

We quickly jump into two cars and make our way to Littleton. On our way I keep an eye out for Jay's car. The roads are completely clear. I start to get nauseous as I think about the possibility of Jay not being around anymore. I keep getting horrible thoughts in my head about how I will find out he's dead and it's all my fault. Gemma was right but I couldn't think of another way to do it.

We arrive at the little Victorian town and I already know something isn't right. It is six thirty and the place is deserted, not a single person in the street. All the shops and pubs are shut, windows boarded up, no lights on, just a load of mist covering the high street. It's literally a ghost town.

"Search the area, head to toe. Leave no stone unturned!"

I walk up the street and look to the floor to see some burn marks. I stand in the middle of a massive circle that has been burnt into the ground, one huge straight burn mark either side. They know his blind spots. How strange. The only people who know of his blind spots are those he trains with. They sometimes use it to their advantage. I look around the village

"JAY!" I shout for him, hoping he will answer.

"JAY!" I shout as loud as I can but I have nothing.

"MY LORD!" One of my soldiers grabs my attention.

They have found his car. I stop in front of it and see the windows have been smashed. I look at the tyres and notice that they have been slashed. All the other soldiers come running to the car. I start to slowly panic as if I can't breathe. I lean up against the car and place my hands on my knees to try and catch my breath. I feel like I have run a marathon.

My captain, William, walks up to me. "My lord, what do we do?"

I look up at him as he gives me support to stand. I stare at the soldiers behind him who are all waiting for my order. I know that I need to get some help. I definitely can't do this on my own.

"We go to the water nation. We need to find him."

I make sure all of my soldiers get into the car safely, then I take one more look around. I take a gulp and try my best to hold back the tears. I get in the back of the car and tears start streaming down my face.

"Are you okay, my lord?"

I nod while looking out the window.

"My lord, he is going to be okay. It's Jay – he's basically unkillable." He's not wrong, but even so, Gemma was still right.

Gemma

I sit at the dinner table in anticipation, awaiting news from Daniel. It is seven p.m. and I have heard nothing.

I can't stop thinking about what Jay said to me before he left: "Gemma, please look after him." That is still going through my head. I look down at my plate and can hardly touch my food; I don't even feel that hungry.

"My lady, you have hardly touched your food."

I look at Frank then at his plate: it is completely empty.

"Just thinking about this whole situation."

He looks at me, concerned. "My lady, all you could do was put your opinion forwards, nothing more. Unfortunately, the fire nation don't really listen to other people's opinions. They are very proud people that like to keep a strong reputation." He's not wrong.

"What do I do, Frank? Sometimes they do need to listen. I would never do that to you."

He smiles. "What you need to remember, my lady, is that Jay and Daniel have been raised together. They know each other inside out and unfortunately before Valdameir got involved they didn't have the best role model in the world."

Valdameir did say something about the previous general. "The previous general – what was his name?"

He wipes his mouth then leans his elbows on the table "Charles Knight. Horrible man never deserved the title of general." Charles Knight. I know that name from somewhere. "I don't know what he did that was so wrong but the British water nation evacuated and came to Russia. Valdameir told Ivan to stay in Russia, told him that this is a fire nation war, that the water nation must not get involved."

I am even more interested in this story.

"What happened to him?"

Frank looks at me as if he is questioning himself. "No one knows. Valdameir came back and never said a word. He spoke to Ivan, of course, but other than that he never said a thing."

I raise an eyebrow, confused. "So no one knows whether he is dead or alive?"

He shakes his head. "Daniel and Jay might but Valdameir definitely does."

I look down at my plate, still not even remotely hungry.

"My lady, I'm going to retire for the night. Do you mind?"

I smile. "Of course not; I will be too. Have a good sleep."

He smiles and kisses me on the forehead. I thank the maids then make my way to my room. I enter my room and close the door; none of my soldiers walk in without knocking so I tend to leave it unlocked. I walk over to the wardrobe and open up the drawer with all my night gowns in. I could do with one making me feel better. I look through and toss ones on the floor that I don't like. I finally find one that I would say is very sexy – black lace, see-through. Thankfully, I am wearing a black lace thong so it should go perfectly. I strip off and place on my night gown. I look in the mirror and admire how amazing it makes me look. Like the other one it shows all my curves, only this one shows a lot more cleavage and a lot more bum. I must admit, I think I have found a new favourite.

Before I know it the doors fly open. I grab my dressing gown which I all of a sudden realise is actually see-through. Daniel walks in. Well, this is embarrassing. He grins, releasing what he has just walked in on.

"Jesus Christ, Daniel!"

His face drops and I notice he has been crying.

"He's gone, they took him!"

I knew this would happen. I run over to him and throw my arms around him. I know how much Jay means to him. He buries his head in my neck and wraps his arms around my waist and sobs. I must admit it feels amazing to be in his arms even if I am half naked. I pull away from him slightly and look at him.

"Go take a seat by the fire. I will get you a drink."

He nods and makes his way over to the fire. I look at one of my soldiers. "Can you get me two glasses and a bottle of rum, please." He bows and heads off.

I catch my soldier staring at one of the fire nation soldiers who is giving me an evil glare. My soldier moves over to where I am standing and continues watching him. "Have we got a problem here?"

The fire nation soldier looks at me square in the eyes. "Not at all, my lady."

My soldier comes back with the two glasses and the bottle of rum I requested.

"Watch him." They nod and stand at either side the door.

I close the door and lock it for safe keeping. I walk over to Daniel, pour him a drink and hand it to him. I pour myself one and sit opposite him.

"Is everything all right?"

I nod. "Of course. Just my soldiers being over-protective." He smiles and wipes his eyes. "So what happened?"

He looks at me, tears still streaming down his face. "It reached about six p.m. and Jay still hadn't come home. I started to get a bad feeling so I went to Littleton where he was." I sit and listen. "It was dead, not a single person in sight, shops and pubs were closed, everything. I knew something wasn't right." It already sounds dodgy to me. "I walked up the street and saw burn marks on the floor. There was a fight but you could tell they knew Jay's blind spots from the positions the burn marks were in." I am more and more curious. "We found his car and the tyres were slashed, the windows were smashed. Someone knew who he was; someone knew he was going to be there."

I take sip of my drink then place it down on the table. "Daniel, how many members of your army can you trust?"

He looks at me, confused and angry. "All of them. I'm their general; I would do anything for those men and they know that."

At this point he is angry. He slams his glass down on the table and stands up.

"My lady, are you okay?"

I look at Daniel. "I'm fine, don't worry."

It goes quiet for a second. "Okay, my lady." My soldiers are clearly on edge about this particular fire manipulator.

"What was that all about? I only slammed a glass on the table."

I look at him, slightly scared, I'm not going to lie. I stand up and come face to face with him. I walk up close to him – we are almost touching. "Like I said, they are just over-protective. One of your soldiers is giving them bad vibes so they are being cautious, that's all."

He moves closer to me. "My soldiers would never hurt you."

I smile. "Good to know, but they need to feel that way, remember. They still feel the need to protect me, plus Ivan probably told each and every one of them to do that."

He smiles and nods. "You're awfully close, my lady."

I take a step back as he is right, I suppose. He slides his hands onto my hips and pulls me in closer. My body is now completely touching his; I can feel his six-pack on my tummy. He smiles at me and then moves in for a kiss. It feels amazing; his lips are so soft. I side my hands up his muscular arms, taking in the feeling of his arms and wrap my arms around his neck. I need to stop but I don't want to stop. He moves his has down to grip my ass. I immediately stop kissing him. He lets go.

"Sorry, I didn't mean to go too far."

I stand there for a moment, dead silent thinking about what just happened.

"I should probably go." He takes a sip of his drink then starts to walk towards the door.

"Daniel, wait!"

He turns round. I walk up to him and place my hand on his cheek and look him in the eyes. He gives me a small smile as he stares at me dead in the eyes. I pull him in for a kiss and he places his left hand on the back of my neck, making the kiss more intense. He uses his right hand to pull me in closer. I run my left hand up his chest then place it on his other cheek, then wrap my arms around his neck. My body is now touching his. His hand slowly moves down my back and stops at the top of my ass but he doesn't touch it. I stop the kiss but still hold him.

"Daniel, I need to tell you something." He looks at me and nods. "I've never done this before."

He pulls me away slightly but still holds me. I sigh and look down in sadness and slight shame.

"Seriously?" He looks shocked.

I nod, preparing for him to let go and walk out. He kisses me on the forehead and tucks my hair behind my ear. "Are you sure you're ready?"

I look down at myself. "Does it hurt?"

He grins. "I wouldn't know. I'm a guy." I take a gulp and nod. "Are you a hundred percent sure?"

I nod. "I will go as easy as I can, but remember, I'm fire nation – I can't promise that I will be able to control myself."

I nod. "I understand." I take a deep breath, knowing that tonight is going to be my first time and it's with a fire manipulator of all people.

He nods. He slowly goes in for another kiss. I'm nervous, yeah, but I'm ready. I start to unbutton his shirt and open it slightly so I can feel his chest. I trace his six-pack with my fingers but notice something. He stops and looks at me. "Every scar tells a story." He grabs the bottom of my night gown and pulls it over my head. He looks down at my body and notices my scars. He traces the one on my breast with his thumb. "Every scar tells a story, right?" He leans down to kiss it. "Will you tell me one day?"

I place my forehead on his. "Only if you tell me yours."

I fully remove his top, which reveals all of his scars and I can't explain what I see. "One day." I trace a particular scar on his shoulder. It is very deep and infected. I get a small vision of him in a cell chained up naked and crying. I look at him, shocked. He watches me as I stare back at it. "It's not a nice story."

From what I briefly saw, clearly not. I move down to one on his chest. It is huge; it goes right across his nipple. He places his hand on mine. "Whatever the story, I'm sure it wasn't your doing." He shakes his head. I smile at him and kiss it. "Just proves how strong you really are."

He smiles at me and pulls me close so our naked body are touching. I start to feel this connection, this strange feeling.

"Kiss me."

He kisses me. I feel a strange surge of power radiating off of me as we kiss. He walks me over to the bed and pushes me down onto it. He pulls off my pants and throws them across the room. He remains at the end of the bed and starts to kiss my vagina. Oh god, that feels amazing.

"Oh, Daniel." I move my hands down to grip his hair as he continues to kiss it. I suddenly feel his tongue in. "Ah." Oh god wow that feels good. I can feel this tingly feeling moving down my body.

He stops and kisses up my body and faces me. He grips one of my breasts and starts to kiss and suck my neck. He places his hand down next to me and starts to move his other hand down my body to my vagina and places two fingers inside me. I moan in his ear and he moves his fingers in and out quicker and quicker, harder and harder. It feels amazing. Doing it myself was one thing but when he does it, it feels a hundred times better. Just his touch makes my body go weak.

He stops then gets up. He drops his trousers and I see it. My eyes widen in shock at how big it is but when I look up at his eyes, I notice they are bright red – is that normal?

"You ready?"

I nod. He lies on top of me and thrusts it in.

"AH!" Fucking hell, that hurt!

He stops for a minute as I grip the skin on his shoulder. He moans in pain – I feel so bad. His eyes go back to the beautiful brown eyes I know. "I'm sorry, I didn't mean to hurt you." He smiles and kisses me. He rests his head on my forehead. "You okay?"

I nod. He starts moving in and out slowly then his eyes go red again and he starts to move faster and faster and pound me harder and harder. It feels amazing; the surge of power within me comes out and I grip him so hard I draw blood. "Harder!"

He is pounding me so hard I must have orgasmed about six or seven times already. The strength within me shows itself. I hold him so close to me I could break something. Blood is dripping off his back.

"Oh, Gemma, yes!"

He intensely kisses me and pulls on my hair. We are both moaning so load I'm sure the whole house can hear us. Daniel eventually slows down and his eyes go back to normal. He pulls out then looks at me. "That was probably the best sex I have ever had."

I laugh. He notices the blood that is pouring on the bed from his back. "Sorry, I don't know what happened, I just felt stupidly strong."

He looks at me and smiles. "Me too, you're not alone on that one." He wasn't just strong; his eyes literally went red.

He gets up and pulls up his pants. "It was a pleasure to be your first, my lady." I smile at him he climbs back on top and kisses my breasts. His eyes went rgoed again and we go for round two.

Water Nation Soldier 1

I hear the moans and groans of the two generals and grin at Jake, my fellow soldier; we knew this would happen, it was just a case of when. They are both young and new generals. Every soldier in the army would die for her because we know she would die for us.

I look to my right and look at the fire nation soldier stood opposite the door. He looks angry. Jake and I have been watching him for the past two hours. Something is a bit dodgy about him but I can't put my finger on it – it is just the way he looks at Gemma and the way he looks at his own general as if he is dirt. Jake and I noticed it not long before Gemma opened the door to request the drinks.

A few more soldiers join us and also can't stop grinning. The dodgy soldier sighs then goes into the great hall. I look at John and the other soldiers then at the other fire nation soldier who I believe is called William.

"You two stay here – I will go and see what's going on." I would but I don't trust him. "Stay here."

I stay back a little but go close enough that I can still hear what's going on. "Now is the time to do it." Do what? "He's done it, hasn't he?" Done what? "Yes, he's shagged her." Oh dear, what's wrong with it? "I knew he was weak and that she was a distraction." Weak? From what I have heard about him he is actually quite strong. He is just young and unmarried; he has a free will to shag whomever he pleases. "The water nation made a grave mistake making her general anyway." The number of times I have heard that statement. She is definitely not weak, that's for sure. I saw her train this morning with Frank; she kicked his ass, made it look easy as well.

William turns and sees me. "I said to stay outside the room!"

I laugh at him slightly. "No offence, but you're on my turf now and it is my job to keep her ladyship safe."

He shrugs and I continued to listen. "It's either him or her ladyship."

My eyes widen. I have heard enough. I go to back to Jake and the others. They clearly have instincts as well.

William follows behind and they all stare at him and give him the evils. "Sounds like they are planning an attack of some kind."

Jake looks at me, concerned and rightly so. "What's the plan?"

I look at him. "Fill the great hall with water nation soldiers. That way they can't get away with hurting her. Wake up the co-general; he has to be told."

He agrees with me then spreads the word. "The great hall is being filled with soldiers now." I nod but my question is who would they be stupid enough to go for Daniel or Gemma?

Frank

I pace my room thinking about all the questions Gemma has asked me about Charles. What if she asks me more – what do I say?

"All you have to do is keep her safe, that is what I hired you to do."

I take a gulp. A rather large man – short dark brown hair, dark brown eyes, cheeky expression – sits in the corner of my room playing with his dagger.

"New toy?"

He grins at it. "It is, actually. I had it professionally made." He carves CM into the table.

"I'm keeping her as safe as I can."

He laughs. I look at him, confused. He walks up behind me, comes up close, to the point I can feel his breath on my neck. He uses the tip of the dagger to move my hair around. "So why is she sleeping with that pathetic excuse for a fire manipulator?"

My eyes widen. "What?"

He leans on my shoulders. "You think I'm not watching? I may be paying you to protect her but I am still always watching."

I take a massive gulp. "I'm sorry my lord. I will try and end it, I promise."

He laughs, comes up in front of me and leans up against the chest of drawers. "Oh please, I have watched her grow up. She lives up to her family name." I raise an eyebrow, trying to decide if that's creepy or not. "My niece is complicated. If Valdameir can't tame her, do you really think you will make a difference?" He does have a good point. "Just like her uncle." He grins.

I roll my eyes. "Oh please, she is more like her father. What's bothering me is all these questions about Charles."

He lets out a little laugh and walks up closer to me. "As she is currently sleeping with one of his lovers, I am sure she will find out eventually. But Charles already knows where he stands with Gemma."

I laugh and rub my temples. "Victims, you mean – we both know that he wasn't Charles's lover."

He shrugs and pours himself a drink. "Whatever. I couldn't give a fuck. The only person that matters to me is Gemma. If he touches her, he dies – simple as that." Charles always finds a way, that is the problem. "I know what you're thinking. Charles always finds a way." I pour myself a drink and sit on the chair opposite the fire place. "You know as well as anyone if he hurts her, I will find him."

I shrug in agreement he sits in the other seat on the other side of the table and puts his feet up. "Don't you think it's a bit creepy watching your niece?"

He sniggers. "Nope. She's family – the only member I care about." I laugh and shake my head. "Laugh all you want, Frank, at least you were brought up in a stable household."

I roll my eyes. "What? My brother and father can't stand me and my mother is dead." I take a sip of my drink

"Boohoo, cry me a river." He raises his eyebrows.

"I'm only well off because of you."

He raises his glass. I smile and raise my glass. We sit there talking about the old days for a bit then there is a knock at the door.

"Who is it?" There is a short pause.

"Jake, my lord."

I get up. "Wait a minute." I turn to him give him a bro hug. "Just keep her safe for me." I smile at him.

"Always."

He climbs out the window and I watch him walk off.

"Come in."

The soldier walks in and looks concerned. "What is it?"

He gulps. "We have a feeling the fire nation soldiers are planning an attack."

My eyes widen. "When?"

He shrugs. "We don't know when or where but her ladyship was mentioned."

I grab my sword and a fresh top. "Just focus on Gemma, no one else; keep her alive. The last thing I need is Clive on my back." He looks at me funny. "I mean Valdameir – don't ask me where I got that from." He nods. "Fill the great hall with soldiers." He nods and walks off.

I fucked up slightly there. I look down at my tattoo, a moon and crossed swords with a wave underneath and CM on either side. I look to the window then make my way to the great hall.

Daniel

"Well, that was fun." She smiles at me I walk over to her wrap my arms around her waist and kiss her on the lips. She laughs a little.

"Daniel, can I ask a question?"

I nod I place my forehead on hers.

"Do your eyes usually go red when you're having sex?"

I look at her, confused. What the hell is she talking about 'red'? She nods at me.

"I have no idea. It's the first time I have been asked that question." Now I think about it the rush of power I had was crazy; I felt like I was about to take off. "Did I hurt you then?"

She shakes her head. "It felt amazing. I was just wondering if you had." She goes into her wardrobe and puts on a less revealing night gown. She still looks sexy, mind you.

I grin. "Do you usually walk around in sexy outfits like you did tonight?"

She grins as she is doing up her dressing gown. I lie on her bed as she lies on top of me. "It makes me feel good."

I bite my lip. "It makes you look good too."

She grins. I tuck her hair behind her ear then run my fingers through it. "You're so beautiful, you know that?"

She grins as she continues to trace a few of my scars; for some reason she seems to like doing that. I kiss her. We start to make out a little then I stop.

"I best get going."

She gives me a sad face. I grin, sit up and pick her up off the bed then put her down slowly. "Thank you for offering to help me find Jay."

She smiles. "How do you know that was an offer?"

I smile at her, still holding her in my arms. I don't want to let go. "Because you wouldn't have done that if you weren't going to help."

She laughs as I move in for another kiss. I pull her in closer and she wraps her arms around me. I stop the kiss. She grins. "Come on, get dressed. I will see you out."

I quickly get dressed and open the door. We walk out and she notices five water nation soldiers grinning at her. "What?"

I grin as well, knowing why they are grinning. "Nothing, my lady, just glad you had fun."

I crack up laughing. She smiles and shakes her head – "Boys." – then rolls her eyes. I walk towards the great hall and notice a strange number of water nation soldiers in the great hall. They are all glaring at my soldiers.

"Do you usually have this many soldiers in the great hall at this time of night?"

She looks around and smiles. "Like I said, over-protective. And you never know what's round the corner." I smile. "You're all doing a fabulous job." She smiles at them.

She looks so proud of them, you can tell that she was made for this role. "Right, boys, we best be off – her ladyship has agreed to help us find your co-general."

I smile, however I do not get one smile back which is strange. I look at William who is also glaring at them funny but I shrug it off slightly. "Okay, well then, thank you, my lady, and I will see you in the morning."

We walk out the door and get into the cars.

"Have fun, my lord?" William, my captain, smiles at me.

"What makes you say that?"

He laughs. "The massive grin on your face."

I smile and replay everything that happened tonight in my head; what it felt like to have her close to me, her smile, how it felt to be inside her. It literally was the best sex I have ever had! More to the point, I can't believe it was her first time.

"It's good to finally see a smile on your face."

He isn't wrong. The only time I ever smile is when I am talking about the old times with Jay, despite what we went through. Suddenly William slams on the brakes.

"Why have we stopped?"

William looks in front of him and takes a gulp. "My lord we have a long line of fire nation soldiers in the way."

Wait, what? I get out the car and see a line of soldiers from my army away from their posts and blocking the road. "What are you doing?" None of them move. "Get back to your posts!" Still none of them move. I start to get angry. "I SAID GET BACK TO YOUR POSTS!"

William gets out of the car. "I don't think any of them are going to move, my lord."

One starts to charge at me, followed by another. I grab the first by the neck, clench my fist and punch him so hard my hand goes through his body. A surge of power goes through my body and fire starts pouring out of my hands. I lift my left arm and open my fist. A tonne of fire is released from the palm of my hand but they keep coming.

"ENOUGH!" I slam my fists down on the floor and fire takes over the ground, burning my men alive. "WHAT THE FUCK IS GOING ON HERE?"

I am so angry I can feel the fire within me coming out. My

whole body is starting to light up. I feel so angry I literally can't control it. Then I feel a large object enter my body.

I look down and see that a spear has been pierced through me from behind. I slowly start to hyperventilate as I am processing the fact I have just been impaled. I fall to my knees and see someone walk in front of me.

"Obvious, isn't it. Your army is turning against you."

I look up and see Phillip, one of my lead guards. "Why? What have I done to deserve this?"

He laughs. "You're weak, Daniel." He pulls the spear out of me. I squeal out in pain as he pulls out the spear. "Charles Knight was so much better than you; he knew what the fire nation stood for."

I hold my wound, as I am still in pain. I look up at him, furious. "Charles Knight was pure evil; he knew nothing about the fire nation or what it stood for."

He laughs and pokes me with the blade then reopens one of my scars. "And yet here we are begging to have him back." I start to become weak, my hands become so hot it starts to melt the ground beneath me. "The old days were so much fun, Daniel. Remember the old days, how close me, you Charles and Jay were." I shake my head and start to get flash backs of the torture.

"He tortured me and Jay. He put us through hell!" I look to William who is being held down by two soldiers.

"As soon as you slept with that slut it just proved you are weak." I feel a rush of anger. Fire comes pouring out my back. "All we had to do was get you as far away from the water nation as possible so we could carry out our plan. You and the co-general are finished."

I start to feel a drop of water on my face and Phillip is looking up, terrified.

"Shame it wasn't far enough."

I see Frank and a load of soldiers charge through the tidal wave that Gemma has created. William runs over to me.

"MY LORD!" I grip hold of William and accidentally burn his neck. "My lord, hang on." I start to close my eyes.

Gemma

I walk Daniel out to the great hall where his soldiers are waiting for him and I notice a lot of my soldiers have made their way into the great hall. They all have worried looks on their faces.

"Do you usually have this many soldiers in the great hall at this time of night?"

No, but something is wrong. My soldiers wouldn't do this unless something wasn't right. "Like I said, over-protective. And you never know what's round the corner." I hope Daniel will catch on. "You're all doing a fabulous job." I smile at all of my soldiers then notice in the distance Frank is up and he doesn't look very happy.

"Well, boys, we best be off; her ladyship has agreed to help us find your co-general." He does not get one smile from his soldiers. I look at my soldiers and they are moving closer and closer. "Okay, well then, thank you, my lady, and I will see you in the morning."

They walk out the door and get into their cars. I shut the door and look round at all the soldiers. "What do I need to know?"

Frank approaches me. "My lady, Jake woke me and said Dean heard some disturbing conversations the fire nation soldiers were having."

Dean steps forwards. "Indeed, my lady, they were saying now is the time or something and that he's weak.," I look at Dean incredibly concerned. "We thought it was best to fill the hall with soldiers just in case they try anything."

I nod then remember what Daniel said. "Someone knew who he was."

I look at the door. "They aren't after me, they are after Daniel."

Frank looks at me. "What shall we do, my lady?"

I look at Frank. "We save him. If 'the time is now', they are going to attack tonight."

Frank and the soldiers smile. "The fire nation is all about pride, yeah, but they clearly aren't smart."

Jake steps forwards. "Then what are we waiting for? Let's go and kick the fire nation's butt."

I smile and we all head out the door. We go on foot just in case. We approach the road just outside the fire nation house. Daniel is on the floor, clearly injured. I look at the soldier stood over Daniel. I look at the scene around him and there is fire everywhere; trees are burning, bushes have been fried, burn marks all over the floor. I suddenly hear a name.

"Charles Knight was so much better than you; he knew what the fire nation stood for." He laughs in Daniel's face.

"Charles Knight was pure evil; he knew nothing about the fire nation or what it stood for."

Why would they want him back? If I know one thing about Valdameir it's that he doesn't go to war for fun.

"And yet here we are, begging for him back." I look at Frank who looks just as concerned as I do. I need to speak to Valdameir. "The old days were so much fun, Daniel. Remember how close me, you, Charles and Jay were?"

Wait? How close were Daniel and Charles?

"He tortured me and Jay. He put us through hell." Oh my god, the scars.

"As soon as you slept with that slut it just proved you are

weak." That's a bit harsh – I'm hardly a slut. "All we had to do was get you as far away from the water nation as possible so we could carry out our plan. You and the co-general are finished."

I clench my fists. Okay, now I'm pissed off.

I run out into the road, flatten my palms, raise one above my head and another across my stomach, put one foot out in front of me and a massive tidal wave of water comes over me. "Shame it wasn't far enough."

Frank and all my soldiers come running through the wave of water, clashing into the fire nation soldiers. I move my arms so quickly in front of me the wave goes past me and all my soldiers and picks up all the soldiers fighting against mine. The fire nation soldiers look at me in fear as I stand there with my palms flat, looking at all of them run for their lives, including the asshole that is standing over Daniel. He looks at me square in the eyes. I push once more and the water turns into a wall of ice to protect my soldiers from the current threat of the fire nation. I slowly lower my hands and my soldiers give me a shocked look.

Frank walks over to me. "You okay, my lady?" I look at him and walk over to the soldier holding Daniel in his arms. I kneel down beside him and feel for a pulse but there is nothing there. I start to cry hysterically. Frank kneels down next to me. Water from the wall starts to float though the air. "My lady, calm down."

I place my hand on Daniel's. "OUCH!" His hands are roasting hot. I look at Frank. "Is that normal?" He shrugs. "Dean, sounds weird, but touch that fire manipulator's hands."

He looks at me and raises an eyebrow. He touches his hand. "Hot?" He shakes his head.

"Daniel's still alive! We need to get him back to the house but be careful – don't burn yourself." My soldiers carry Daniel off carefully back to the house. I stand there in the middle of the road looking at the wall of ice. The fire nation soldier looks at me.

"My lady what do we do?"

I look at him then to Frank. "Send of a request to the Russians. I need them here; I need to speak with Valdameir."

He looks at me. "You know what Valdameir is like when you ask too many questions."

I smile. "He practically raised me. He won't hurt me."

Frank starts to walk off.

"Frank," he stops and looks at me, "send off another message." He looks at me, confused. "To Dan Val Gule."

The fire nation soldier looks at me in shock. Frank and my soldiers freeze. "My lady, he is the most feared and most dangerous fire manipulator in the world. Are you sure?"

I look at the soldier. "What's your name?"

He looks at me. "William, my lady?"

I smile at him. "Well, William, I need answers and the only two people who can give those to me are Valdameir and Dan Val Gule."

I turn to Frank who quickly approaches me. "My lady, I'm sure Valdameir can answer all your questions."

I look at Frank with a serious look. "No, he can't. I have different questions for Dan Val Gule."

William laughs. "Well, my lady, I hands-down respect you; you're a brave woman."

I start to walk back to the house. "He won't hurt me or my army."

Dean jumps in. "How do you know that?"

I give him a small grin. "Because he will regret it if he does."

Since having sex with Daniel, I have never felt more alive. I have never felt so strong. It was like a flick of a switch.

"Above all, we need to find Jay." I look at the members of my army I brought with me and they all smile at me including Frank. "Frank."

He walks up to me and bows. "On it, my lady." And he goes off to send my messages. Whoever is behind this – if they want a war, I will give them one.

Jay

I slowly open my eyes and my head is pounding. I look around trying to get my eyes to adjust but in the mean time I turn to my other senses.

The smell of this place is horrendous; I am either in a farm or a morgue. I can't really make out the smell because there is so many going up my nose it's actually frying my nose hair. I touch the ground with my hand and feel some hay and mud: I'm in a farm. I must be.

I push myself up and I am now starting to see clearly and I am not going to lie I am a little bit on the cold side. My vision returns and I notice I am in a cage in the middle of a camp. Well, this is not good. I see three other men sat in the same cage as me. One is so skinny you can see his bones. His hair was dark but due to the condition he is in it's losing its colour. One is a big boy with short ginger hair and icy blue eyes. The last is another skinny one with short, light blonde hair who looks like he is contemplating life. I can't say I blame him. I look back at the dude that is skin and bones.

"Is he still alive?" The last thing I want is to be sat in a cage with a dead body.

"We don't know; he's been like that for days."

That's a yes then. I give him a small poke and he moves slightly. "He's still with us."

The big boy looks at me, terrified.

"Where are we?"

He shrugs. "We have no idea. We move about all the time."

Oh Jesus Christ. "At least we aren't alone, right?"

The guy with the blonde hair looks at me. "Oh please, what could be worse than this? We could die any second. They do love abusing us."

Well, he has a point, in a way. "I have been in a situation a lot worse, trust me."

They all stare at me in shock. "Really? Did the general save you?"

I raise my eyebrow. "A general saved me, yeah, but not the British one – he was going through it as well." Their eyes widen. "What're your names?"

The big boy speaks first: "Peter."

I look at the blonde one. "Robert, but you may call me Rob."

I look at the skinny dude. "What's his name, do you know?"

Rob faces me. "I believe his name is Steve." Well, poor Steve won't be alive for much longer if we don't sort him out quick.

A few soldiers walk up to the cage and open it up.

"He's awake." I know this guy from somewhere.

"I am. Who are you?"

He grins. "Surprised you don't recognise me."

Then it clicks. "Preston, of course. What other asshole would it be." I have never liked Preston and he has never liked me.

"Nice nap, my lord?"

I grin. "Yeah, I guess, but I seem to have moved location somehow. Can't think how or why."

Peter looks at me, registering who I am.

"Keep your sarcastic comments to yourself; he's on his way."

Who's on his way? "And who might that be?"

He walks out and shuts the door. I smile at him. I lean against the bars of the cage.

"You're a lord?"

I nod. "Co-general of the fire nation."

His eyes widen. "I have heard stories about you, my lord. Weird ones, actually." I smile.

The soldiers then come in with another man, wearing a strange kind of uniform. Definitely water nation, which is strange. It's old uniform with a wave symbol on the arm, definitely not a general or co-general. They throw him in the same cage as us and he lands in my lap, head-butting me straight in the balls. I squeal in pain.

"Sorry." He sits up swiftly. He has sort dark brown hair and dark brown eyes.

"It's cool."

He smiles. "What's your name?"

I smile back. "Jay." He leans up against the railings opposite me. "What about you?"

He looks a little saddened. "Charlie."

He curls up into a little ball I smile at him. "How did you end up here? You're water nation?"

He looks at me. "Yeah, well, I'm not exactly a normal water manipulator."

I laugh. "I'm not a normal fire manipulator. There we go, we have something in common already." He laughs. I feel weirdly comfortable around him which is a bit rare for me. "o where do you come from?"

He smiles. "Nowhere special. You?"

I laugh. "Me neither. I don't actually know where I come from."

His smile drops. "Oh well. We are both still alive, right?"

He's like a water nation version of me.

"Damn straight. I do love my weird and wonderful adventures."

He grins. "You sure do meet some interesting people."

I laugh. "You sure do."

I smile at him. I feel like I know him but I can't think where from. Either that, or we have a strange connection. He has quite a warm smile and I can't take my eyes off his until I notice a tattoo on his arm: a moon and four dots leading down to a wave. Weird, I have never seen a water manipulator with a tattoo. I am pretty sure they are against them actually.

"Cool tattoo."

He covers it up pretty swiftly. "Oh yeah, me and my brothers just went on the piss one night and it ended with a tattoo."

I laugh. "Classic night out then." He laughs and looks worried. "Hey, your secret is safe with me." He smiles. "Besides, we probably won't ever see each other again after this."

He laughs. "That's a shame."

He smiles at me I return the smile. Preston comes in again and grins. "That's a nice big smile, Jay. You excited?"

I raise my eyebrows. "For what? I don't even know why I'm here."

He laughs. "We have been assigned to collect and deliver you to someone special." I gulp, only thinking of one person. "Relax, it's not him, but when he does get back into power and he has both you and Daniel back..." He grins, walks up to me and stands over me. "Just the right level – I still remember how good you were."

I gulp. He strokes my face. I look over at Charlie who is watching and processing what is going on with one eyebrow raised. Preston strokes my cheek he starts to unbuckle his trousers then an arrow pierces him straight through the head. I have never felt more relieved in my life.

Charlie and I both stand up. An army of fire manipulators come flying through the camp taking out every soldier. They basically overwhelm them. Fire is pouring through the camp, throats are being slit and heads are being removed from bodies. Impressive for a rogue army.

A soldier opens the cage and grabs all of us, including dead-man Steve. We walk through the camp, which has been completely destroyed. We are presented in front of a man with tall light brown hair, a big muscular guy with, from the looks of it, major anger issues. He stands there with his back to us.

"They had prisoners, my lord."

He sighs. "Great." God, he sounds happy…not! "Do any of them have a trade?"

All of them nod, including Charlie. I just stare at him, registering how big this guy actually is!

"All of them accept one, my lord." He pauses for a second. "However, one of them is a water manipulator." Meaning Charlie.

"Give him a horse and let him go."

Charlie is uncuffed and given a horse.

"See ya. I will see if I can get a ticket to your funeral."

I smile. "Cheeky cunt. Who says I want you there? See ya."

He smiles and rides off into the distance.

"Anyone who is close to death, put them out of their misery. The one that hasn't got a trade, kill him."

Ha, he thinks he's funny. The soldier comes towards me.

"Excuse me, angry man." The soldier stops and looks at him in disbelief. "I think I have the right to know who is going to be executing me, don't you?"

He turns round and I gulp so hard my Adams apple could have fallen straight through my asshole.

"Oh, I'm fucked."

He smiles. "Seems like you know exactly who I am."

I lower my head, sigh then look back up to him. "The Ripper – yes, I know exactly who you are. The second most wanted man in the world."

He walks up closer to me. He is twice the size of me. "And you are?"

Well, I'm going to die anyway so I may as well tell him. "I'm Jay, co-general of the Great British fire nation army. You can either take my word for it or risk a letter to the general, up to you."

He stands there with a massive grin on his face. "You're a general?"

I roll my eyes. "Co-general, I just help the general, ya know."

He looks at his army. "Hear that, boys! We have a lord! Kill him."

I stand there waiting to die as he watches. I look up at him to give him a warning. "He won't be happy."

He laughs at me. "Who? Your general? When have generals ever done me any favours anyway?" He turns to his army. "Hear that? His general won't be happy." They all laugh. "The last general that picked on me and my family is brown bread."

I look at him square in the eyes. "And who might that be? Because I can think of several. I know one who isn't stupid enough, but we will see." He sighs and gives his soldier the signal to just do it. "My general's name is Daniel."

The soldier pauses mid-way and the Ripper freezes. All the soldiers look at each other. The Ripper looks at me so angry that at this point I am borderline terrified.

"That's not funny." He picks me up with both hands by my coat.

"What? I'm serious, his name is Daniel."

He drops me and I fall on my back. Fucking hell, that hurt.

"His name is Daniel, you say?"

I look at the Ripper who is so tense that all of his muscles are showing. "Yep." I am lying there in agonising pain. "Known him for eighteen years, I think I would know his name."

He turns and glares at me as I painfully get up. "Send a message off to my brother – tell him it's urgent – and get this guy a horse." He lifts me up onto a horse then the dragon figure falls out my pocket.

"Wait!" I pretty much fall off the horse to get it back. When I pick it up, I notice the dragon's eyes are open. That's strange, I could have sworn they were closed.

He picks me up again and places me back on the horse. "Nice dragon. Like them, do you?" He gives me a warm fatherly smile this time.

"Yeah, me and Daniel have always wanted one."

He looks at me seriously. "What if you have always been around one?" What the fuck is he talking about? "My name is Richard, by the way."

I was not expecting him to have the most basic name known to man. "I wasn't expecting that name, I'm not going to lie."

He laughs. "Don't worry, I'm not a monster really, I just enjoy killing people."

I laugh. "Same." We both start riding. "Where are we, by the way?"

He smiles. "Finland."

I look at him, confused. I'm a long way from home.

Richard

"My lord, I have some juicy news for you." I always smile when my right hand man Elijah comes in and says that. "Some soldiers have reported a nearby wanna-be army camp, not far from here."

I look at him and grin. Elijah has a similar body build to me with short black hair and blue eyes – quite a handsome devil really.

"How big of an army?"

He sits at the table in my tent. "Not even half the size of ours."

I haven't had any action in a few weeks. "Sounds juicy. What're we waiting for? Get the men ready."

I get up onto my horse and lead the army to this camp. Upon arrival I can see what Elijah means: what a pathetic excuse for a camp.

"Charge, but leave a few for me."

Elijah gives the order and the men go and have their fun. I watch from the sidelines while my army literally slaughters theirs. It's a shame really. I was hoping it would be bigger. I walk through the burning camp with the biggest smile on my face.

"Did we lose any men?" Elijah smiles I smile back knowing that I won without losing a single man. "Get the men to tidy up after themselves. Where are my victims?"

He leads me over to a line of men. "All camp leaders. I know you like killing the big bosses."

I laugh at him. "Why such a small camp? You must know

that there are people like me out there."

They all stay quiet then I notice something: one of them is wearing a fire nation uniform with the Great British flag on the top of the arm. Their uniform is quite posh: black wrap top with red outlining the fire nation symbol, which is just a small flame, on the right hand side of the chest, long elasticated trousers and boots that go halfway up their shins. You can always tell which country they are from because they have the flag on the top right sleeve.

"You're a long way from home, buddy." He is literally shaking. "What's the matter, cat got your tongue?" These guys are no fun. Elijah forces open his mouth and I grab hold of his tongue. "I guess a dragon has instead." I pull so hard I rip it out of his mouth, then I punch him so hard in the chest I make my way inside and squeeze his heart until it explodes. He falls to the floor. "Save that one. Valayrion needs to eat."

He looks confused "Why that one?"

I look at him. "Look at the type of people he's around. He looks like a traitor to me."

He shrugs and drags him over to a few men. I move over to the next one. "What do they call you?" He also stays quiet. "Elijah, these people are boring, they don't talk."

He grins. "Just kill them then."

I start ripping them to shreds. I pull a few arms out, burn a few.

"They had prisoners, my lord."

I sigh. I fucking hate prisoners. Always so hard done by. "Great." I look at the soldier that brought them out, furious. He gulps. "Do any of them have a trade?" I await a response.

"All accept one, my lord." He looks back at them. "However, one of them is a water manipulator."

The last thing I need is the water nation elders on my back. "Give him a horse and let him go." I turn to Elijah. "Anyone who is close to death, put them out of their misery. The one that doesn't have a trade, kill him."

Elijah moves towards him. I wait for the screams because I know he is just as bad as me.

"Excuse me, angry man." Someone with balls, finally! "I think I have a right to know who is going to be executing me, don't you?"

I smile and turn to face him. He is a small lad with dirty blonde hair, blue eyes and has a cheeky expression. However, he goes from a dragon to a mouse in seconds.

"Oh I'm fucked."

My grin gets even bigger. "Seems like you know exactly who I am."

He lowers his head and sighs like he is admitting defeat. "The Ripper, yes – I know exactly who you are. The second most wanted man in the world." This lad is interesting, I will admit.

"And you are?"

He looks me in the eye. "I'm Jay, co-general of the Great British fire nation army. You can either take my word for it or risk a letter to the general, it's up to you."

Well, well, well, a co-general is in my presence. I should be honoured …not! "You're a general?" Given his size and his attitude, it sort of shocked me a bit; it's like he uses it to survive, which is interesting.

"Co-general. I just help the general, ya know."

I turn to my army and just feel like I have hit the jackpot. "Hear that, boys! We have a lord! Kill him." I stand there and watch as Elijah moves towards him again.

"He won't be happy."

I laugh. "Who? Your general? When have generals ever done me any favours anyway?" I turn to my army again. "Hear that? His general won't be happy." They all laugh as he stands there with a serious look on his face. "The last general that picked on me and my family is brown bread."

He looks at me square in the eyes, I will admit this lad really does have balls. "And who might that be? Because I can think of several. I know one who isn't stupid enough, but we will see." He is starting to annoy me now so I give the nod. "My general's name is Daniel."

I freeze on the spot. My whole army went goes quiet. How dare he mention that name in my presence? "That's not funny." I walk up to him and pick him up by his clothes.

"What? I'm serious, his name is Daniel."

Could it be? I drop him and pace slowly. "His name is Daniel, you say?" I feel so tense but almost nervous.

"Yep." I feel so confused. I need to know more. "Known him for eighteen years, I think I would know his name." Eighteen years? I glare at him so angry and hopeful at the same time.

"Send a message off to my brother – tell him it's urgent – and get this guy a horse." As he was in pain, I had to help him onto his horse.

"Wait!" I noticed a dragon figure fall from his coat pocket. He grabs it and I pick him up and place him back on his horse.

"Nice dragon. Like them, do you?" I give him a kind smile. This time as I have the slightest bit of hope that I have found him

"Yeah, me and Daniel have always wanted one."

I give him a serious look. "What if you have always been around one?" He looks at me extremely confused. "My name is Richard, by the way."

He grins at me. "I wasn't expecting that name, I'm not going to lie."

I laugh. "Don't worry, I'm not a monster really. I just enjoy killing people."

He laughs at me. "Same."

Well, that's comforting, I suppose. I start to ride towards my camp, which thankfully isn't too far away.

"Where are we, by the way?"

I laugh at him. "Finland."

He looks at me dead confused. I grin.

We get to my camp and my soldier stops me. "He hasn't landed yet. What do you want me to do with the body?"

Late as usual. "He will be back shortly, don't worry. Anything for food – you know what he's like."

Jay looks at me so confused. It has just occurred to me that he knows nothing about Valayrion, which is a good thing for the moment because he will be a hungry boy.

I sit at the table in my tent and he just stands there.

"Sit." He gingerly takes a seat in the opposite chair. I pour him a drink and look at him; he looks nervous. "Well, tell me, how do you know him?"

He takes a sip of his drink. "Who?"

That pisses me off slightly, although he seems to be too busy looking round the room. I slam my glass on the table to get his full attention. "Daniel, you twat."

He seems a bit scared. "I'm not telling you anything about him." Over-protective, I can see.

"Okay then, tell me about yourself."

He downs his drink then refills it. "What do you want to know?" He looks at me and raises and eyebrow.

"Where you from?" I light a fire in the fire place as I can see he is starting to get a little cold.

He looks at me, slightly saddened, sits back in his chair and sighs. "I don't know. I don't really know anything about myself." I kinda feel sorry for the kid. I feel like he has had it a bit rough.

"Okay, who raised you and Daniel?"

He sighs then gives a little laugh. He leans forwards in his chair. "A psycho. That's all you need to know."

Interesting. I can think of a few people that could be. "So not a great childhood."

He shakes his head. "Nope, it is a childhood I would rather not talk about."

I raise my eyebrow he might not want to talk about it but I'm intrigued. "Would you tell me one day?"

He shrugs. "The only people that know anything about my childhood are the soldiers, Daniel and Valdameir."

I lean forwards. "Valdameir? Who's that?"

He gave me a little laugh. "Really? You don't know who Valdameir is?" I shake my head, trying to rack my brains on who that could possibly be. "The Russian general." The cogs are turning in my head.

"You know, I didn't have the best childhood either." He looks at me and rolls his eyes. "My father hated me. Loved my brothers, there was just something about me that he didn't like."

He looked at me, confused. "Not surprised you're one of the most wanted men in the world."

I laugh. "Nah, it wasn't that. My brother is more wanted than me and he is still proud." He freezes and stares at me. "Both of my brothers caught him beating the crap out of me one day so we all ran away and lived our best life." He smiles. "We were killing people for fun, drinking, shagging girls, the lot. Those were the good old days. Then we became old and went our sperate ways. One brother fell out with the other and I just stayed out of it."

He laughs. "Old? You can't be that old, surely?"

I look at him and raise my eyebrows. "I'm forty-three."

He looks a tad shocked. "Nah, fuck off, you're not forty-three?" I nod. "Well, that has shocked me a bit. Anyway, me and Daniel use to do that minus the killing. We had no interest in that, we just shagged girls and got drunk. Well, Daniel never got drunk, the lucky sod." I smile at him; I knew opening up to him slightly would work. "Without fail, he would wake me up the following morning with a bucket of ice-cold water."

That is just evil, if you ask me. You should never wake up a man when he is sleeping, especially when he is hungover. "Brutal. Safe to say that has never happened to me."

He looks into the fire. "Lucky you." He starts to shed a tear. "I miss him. I miss *that,* but I wouldn't go back there."

I am a tad confused. "Why not?"

He stares at me. "Because of the man that raised us." Who is this man?

Just as Jay is starting to trust me, Dan Val Gule walks in. Jay jumps out of his skin and bolts to the corner of the room. Dan Val Gule smiles. "That was quick." He sits down and stares at Jay. "You said it was urgent. What is it?"

I stare at him. "I think I have found him." He raises an eyebrow. "Daniel. I think I have found him."

He stands up and looks at Jay. "Richard, he looks nothing like him."

I look at him and snigger. "Not him, you idiot. That's his best friend." He looks at Jay and back at me. "He's the general of the Great British fire nation."

Dan Val Gule falls back into his chair. "This is a problem."

I nod. "Yes, it is."

If Daniel is the general, this is a massive problem.

Gemma

The soldiers carry his near-enough lifeless body into one of the smaller rooms. The extra rooms are pretty much similar to mine but smaller. The bathrooms are the same and they all have a walk-in wardrobe with spare clothes.

The doctors came in to examine him and to hopefully try and save him. They remove all his clothing minus his underwear, revealing all his scars; when the doctor saw them, he looked gob smacked. "The boy really has been through hell," I hear him say. They give the clothes to the maids and they take them away to wash and stitch them up. I walk into my office out of the way and await news.

An hour or two pass and I am starting to get impatient. I get up to go and see what's going on but the doctor walks in.

"My lady, may I talk to you?"

I nod. "Is it about Daniel?"

He nods at me and gives me a sigh. "I apologise, my lady. I had to assess his whole body. Not only does he have the injury from tonight he has several infected scars all over his body." I sit there wanting to cry. "Several of them should have killed him, including the one tonight."

I become slightly tense. "But?"

He sighs. "It seems his power is actually keeping him alive and clearing all the infections."

Now I'm just confused. "That's impossible?"

He shrugs. "I have never known anything like it. He must be

very powerful if his body is fully capable of doing that without a doctor and it concerns me." It is very worrying. "My lady, you need to be careful. Promise me." I nod and he leaves the room. I start to cry, knowing that what happened between me and Daniel was probably a mistake and could have killed him.

"My lady." Frank walks through the door and sits in the chair opposite. "Ivan and Valdameir have arrived."

I look at him. "That was quick."

He nods. "You need to give a speech. The army need to know that the fire nation cannot be trusted."

I pull myself together and make my way to the training grounds where my army is waiting. "Good evening." They all look at me. God, this is a bit scary. "As you may well know, the fire nation army launched an attack on their general this evening. I do not know if the whole army is guilty or just a few, but as of tonight the Great British fire nation is hereby an enemy to the water nation. None of them can be trusted and until their general wakes we must protect the body, we must find their co-general, but above all you need to keep yourselves alive as I will need each and every one of you." I pause for a moment. "We are the water nation of Great Britain! We protect the people of the British water nation! We are the wall between the threat and them! And right now, we have a threat. Will you soldiers of the Great British water nation stand with me? Help me protect the body of the fire nation general so the threat to the water nation disappears so that he can take his place back as general and we can reunite once again!" My whole army cheers and I stand there with pride.

"Well done, my lady."

I smile, my time as the water nation general has officially started.

Jay

Dan val Gule is here right in front of me, the most wanted man in the world the most feared man in the world.

"That was quick." He sits down then stare at me. I am completely speechless, which is a first for me. "You said it was urgent. What is it?"

I stand there listening in. "I think I have found him." He stares at Richard. "Daniel. I think I have found him."

He stands up and looks at me. "Richard, he looks nothing like him." He is still staring at me, giving me an evil glare. I am thinking about my escape route but I literally have nowhere to run.

"Not him, you idiot. That's his best friend." Still looking at me, he sighs, then looks at Richard. "He's the general of the Great British fire nation."

Dan Val Gule falls back in his chair. He looks gutted. "This is a problem." Problem?

"Yes, it is." Okay, I'm just confused now. Richard looks back into the fire.

"Okay, I'm confused. Why do you want Daniel?"

Dan Val Gule looks at me. "It's got nothing to do with you."

Okay, now he and I have a problem. "It has everything to do with me. He is my best friend and I'm not about to let you kill the only person that actually matters to me."

He smiles at me while Richard stares into the fire, drinking. "You have balls boy, I will admit. What makes you think I want to kill him?" He walks up close to me until I can feel his breath on my forehead. He is about six foot two, I would say, with light brown hair and light brown eyes with a very muscular built body just like Richard. However, he is definitely taller than Richard.

For some reason I look to Richard for help. "Leave him alone, Val Gule, he's just a boy."

He doesn't listen to Richard. "You're going to tell me everything you know about your friend, even if I have to squeeze it out of you."

Richard touches him on the shoulder. "If it is him, are you sure you want to start off by killing his best friend?"

I give him an evil grin because Richard has a point. "What is it you want to know exactly?"

He gives me the most emotionless look known to man. "Don't give me that look, boy. I will find out about him either way, but it will just be easier and quicker for you to tell me. How long have you known him?"

I remain quiet and Richard sits back down and stares at me. I look at Dan Val Gule and say nothing. He comes angry very quickly and launches the desk across the room, breaking it.

"I SAID HOW LONG HAVE YOU KNOWN HIM!"

Richard doesn't say a word.

"Eighteen years."

Dan Val Gule stands there, still angry. "Good, now you're getting the message." He moves closer to me. "Now how do you know him?" He calms down slightly.

For my own safety I decide to comply. "We were raised by the British general together."

He paces the room. "Okay, good. Now tell me: where does he come from?"

I look at Richard.

"He's not going to help you in this situation. This affects him as much as it does me." Richard grins and sits back in his chair.

"SPEAK, BOY!"

Fucking hell! I don't think I have ever been so scared.

"ALL RIGHT!" I take a deep breath. Please forgive me, Daniel. "He is from Whitefall. His family kicked him out when he was four and he was taken in by the fire nation general, where we met. Both of us went through hell then the fire nation general went to war against Valdameir, the Russian general. He was defeated then Daniel became general. He is also stupidly strong and can't control his temper lately."

Dan Val Gule walks over to the other side of the room. "I'm convinced, Val Gule. It's him."

I looked at him, terrified.

"Put through hell how?"

I feel like he is angry for another reason now. "Well, we were both abused. It's a long story." He starts breathing heavily and looks at Richard, who is also angry. "What's going on?"

He stares at me. "By who?"

I am about to tell him until I hear a roar come from outside of the tent. "Fuck off, it can't be!"

My attention is elsewhere now. I run out the tent and look to my left and see two of the most beautiful dragons I have ever laid my eyes on. One is medium size, I would say: shiny light yellow scales with a blue stripe with black outlining and a white tummy. The other one is a shiny dark red with black tummy and wings. He is humungous. I walk closer to them but not too close and stop. The yellow one moves slightly closer to me. Its giant head is about the same size as half my body. Looking in closer, it has sapphire blue eyes. I place my hand on his nose and start to stroke him. My dream has finally come true: I am literally stoking an actual dragon.

"His name is Valayrion." I turn round to see Richard, who walks closer to him and strokes him. "He's my best friend, someone I know will never betray me."

Oh my god, he literally owns a fucking dragon.

"You're telling me you own a literal dragon?"

Richard grins. "Well, I wouldn't say I *own* him; he has the same mind as me."

That just confuses me. "How can a dragon have the same mind as you?"

Valayrion is now nudging me. I give him a little cuddle.

"He is basically me but in the form of a dragon."

I am too busy admiring this beautiful creature. "Ever since I was a kid I have always wanted to meet a dragon."

Richard walks closer to me then looks at the other dragon. "That one is Val Gule's. His name is Vision." I look at the massive red one and can see he's not keen on me. "Vision has never been keen on strangers, just like Dan Val Gule. Unless you're Daniel, of course."

I am confused at this point. "Why Daniel?"

Richard walks closer to me. "Daniel is basically his baby. He's Dan Val Gule's son." Oh dear, that's not good. "Hear him out – he's finally found him."

I nod and we go back into the tent for me to hear his story.

Dan Val Gule

As Jay and Richard are outside looking at the dragons, I am still trying to process what I just heard. It is basically identical to my story. I might have actually found him, my son, my boy. I still remember the day I held him in my arms, his tiny little feet, his little chubby body and his brown eyes staring up at me. I was the happiest man alive. I still remember when Richard met him. He was so happy to be an uncle. The day he went missing was the day my soul broke, the day my heart shattered into a million little pieces and now he hates me. I can't help but cry. I have found him and I will never get him back but I know he needs me. He doesn't understand himself or who he is.

Richard and Jay walk back into the tent. "You okay, Val Gule?"

I nod. "Just hard to process."

Jay stands in front of me. "He's your son?" I look at Richard then back at Jay and nod. "I'm willing to hear you out, but I will warn you he will not take this lightly."

I know that. "I know, but if you hear my story you might be able to help him come to terms with it, at least because he needs me."

Jay nods.

"When he was only a few months old, me and Richard had to go off to war so I left him and his mother. I didn't really love her that much but she was the mother of my child so I learned to love her. It was when I got back it all went downhill."

Flashback

"Honey, I'm home."

Pure silence.

"Honey?"

Something isn't right. We only live in a small Victorian town house. It has only a few rooms; the kitchen and the living room are both in the same room. It is only a small kitchen, two or three surfaces and a bog-standard fridge. Small bathroom with a small bath, sink and toilet and above the sink is a small square mirror. Upstairs are two bedrooms, the master bedroom for me and my girlfriend Mary and the nursery, obviously for my son Daniel.

I start to panic as Mary is not answering. I go straight to Daniel's room and find him lying in his cot. He isn't wearing anything and his nappy hasn't been changed. He isn't breathing.

I start to cry. "No, no, please no." He looks dead. I pick up his little lifeless body and cry as I hold my son in my arms. I touch his tiny little hands. "OUCH!" His hands are red hot.

Then it occurs to me: what if he's still alive? I take him over to the changing station and grab a baby-grow and blanket out of the drawers. I reach over to the top of the set of drawers and grab the baby powder, baby wipes and a fresh nappy. Even if Daniel is dead, he isn't going to die like this. I take him to the bathroom and run him a nice hot bath, remove his nappy and put it in the bin – I can't even begin to describe the smell – and pop him gingerly in the bath tub.

I wash his little fragile body until I am convinced he is completely clean. I take him back upstairs to his room to dry him off, put some lotion on him to make his skin silky smooth again, put his nappy on and his nice warm baby-grow, and wrap him up in a blanket, which his hands managed to set on fire. I put it out pretty swiftly and go out the house to find Richard.

I look in every pub until I manage to find him. "Richard." He turns round and looks so happy to see Daniel.

"Oh, there he is, my handsome nephew!" Richard's smile fades when he notices I have been crying. Vision has started to cry as well. "What's wrong?"

I hold Daniel to my chest so tight I won't even let Richard hold him. "Mary's gone. She left Daniel. I don't know how long for but I want her found, Richard. Find her for me." Daniel eventually starts crying in my arms. "He's hungry; I have to fed him. Promise me you will find her."

Richard is fuming. "You have my word."

He turns to a few of his soldiers. "Come on, boys we have a traitor to hunt down."

They all leave the pub and I go to the shop to get some baby food. Daniel is crying. I look at him and feel so guilty for leaving him. I feel like the worse dad in the world. I find some baby food and some food for myself and go back to the house.

I lay Daniel down on the sofa and sort out his food. I hold him in my arms while I gave him his bottle. He stops crying and looks up at me with those big brown eyes.

"It's okay, Daddy's here now. Daddy will always look after you."

After his bottle I burp him then grab myself something to eat. I am starving. I hold him in my arms while he falls asleep, then Richard comes charging through the door and he starts to cry.

"Fucking hell, Richard."

He grins and sits next to me. "It's okay, buddy, it's only uncle Richard." He starts to calm down slightly. "Good news or bad news first?"

I look at him, angry. "Good news?"

He grins. "We found her."

That was quick, but if I know one thing about Richard when it comes to his nephew, I know he will get it done quick.

"Bad news?"

His smile drops. "She was sleeping with another guy and to make it ten times worse she was pregnant with his baby."

Which means she must have left him for a fair few months.

"How far along?"

He looks at me. "Three months." I am so angry. "Come with me."

Unfortunately, I have to take Daniel with me. I'm not about to leave him all by himself. I walk out the door and Mary is in the street with the guy she is sleeping with. I can see the small bump. I come face to face with her, holding Daniel in my arms.

"Why?"

She spits in my face, making Daniel cry. Vision lands behind me, his head coming just over my shoulder. "Shh, not yet, buddy." As I stroke his chin, he glares at her.

"I SAID WHY?"

Daniel is still crying. Valayrion lands next to Vision. "Valayrion, I need you to cuddle Daniel for me." I place Daniel on the floor and Valayrion tucks his wing under him and curls his neck to place his head next to Daniel. He is like a peanut compared to Valayrion's head.

I look back at Mary. "Well?" Richard comes up behind the bloke. "Richard, she needs some encouragement."

He smiles and hit the guy so hard in the chest, he grabs hold of his heart and rips it out.

"NOOO!" She hysterically cries.

"I asked why."

Richard throws his heart in front of her. "Little present for you." He enjoyed that.

"You never deserved a child; you are pure evil!"

Richard and Vision grin. "I don't think I am the evil one here, Mary. What kind of a mother leaves her child to die?" Richard looks at me to hurry me up but he knows what I'm doing. "You can at least just run away with him. I would still find you and still kill you but at least he will be alive." She cries. "Now you know what happens when you mess with the Krane family." I look at Vision. "Go on, boy, take revenge for our boy."

I watch as Vision spits out fire until she is nothing but ashes. I turn to Valayrion, who has calmed Daniel down and put him to sleep, pick up Daniel and look at Richard. "We need to get him somewhere safe."

We find a little town called Whitefall where I find a cute little family. They had already have children. I knock on the door

"Good evening." I think they are intimidated by my build and height. "I need a favour. I'm going off to war and I need you to look after my son while I'm away. I will be back for him."

She takes Daniel in her arms and all of his stuff then nods. I kiss his forehead. "Daddy will be back." I walk away with tears streaming down my face.

Four years later

Today is Daniel's birthday and I'm off to collect him. He is going to be four today and I can't wait to see him. Obviously I didn't want to go home first so my army came with me. Vision was very excited to see him again. I knock on the door of the family's house and the mother opens the door.

"I am here to collect my son."

She looks at me with a frown on her face. "He's not here."

I laugh. "Why, is he out playing or something?" Richard comes up behind me.

"No, we kicked him out."

The rage within me overloaded. "Richard." He and some of my men drag the whole family out of the house and pull them into the middle of the street. My army starts locking people in their houses and the parents are placed in front of me. "Why?"

The mother looks at me, terrified. "He was a freak; fire was coming out of his fists."

Vision comes down behind me and start questioning where Daniel is – he was looking everywhere. "They kicked him out, buddy."

Vision goes mental. He flies in the air then starts to burn the houses with everyone in them. He starts to destroy the whole town and I have no intention to stop him.

"See what happens when you kick out A FOUR-YEAR-OLD BOY!"

They watch as their home town is being burnt down by Vision until it is ashes. Richard also just stands there and watches it happen. "Did it not occur to you that maybe, just maybe, if Daniel has special abilities, maybe his father does too?"

Valayrion decides to join in the fun. They watch both of the dragons fly around destroying their village as well as a village near-by.

"This is all on you; you kicked out his baby so anything he destroys, it's on you. At the end of the day, he's a dragon. He will destroy if you take away from him what is his." I nod at Richard and he rips apart the father. I place my arms in front of me my eyes turn red and I open my palms. Fire comes pouring out of my palms until them and their family are ashes.

End of Flashback

Jay looks at me in complete and utter shock with tears streaming down his face. "Wait, so his mum hated him and that family kicked him out without the thought that you might be a fire manipulator too, not to mention own a dragon?"

I nod at him. "Wow, that is a really shit life. I don't think he is going to take that all too well."

I lean forwards. "I don't expect him to, but, Jay, if you're telling me he is powerful and he is losing his temper quickly, HE NEEDS ME!" Jay looks down at his drink then takes a sip.

A soldier from my army walks in. "What?" He hands me a scroll. I look at the sticker holding it together. "It's from the water nation general of Great Britain."

Jay spits out his drink. "Well, go on, what does it say?"

I open it up:

Dear Dan Val Gule
Daniel, the fire nation general, is severely injured due to an attempt made on his life by his own men and I was wondering if you could come to the water nation in Great Britain. I have a range of questions I need to ask about him and I feel like you're the only person that can answer them, so please consider my proposal.
Many Thanks
Gemma
General Of The Great British Water Nation Army

I look at the message and become so angry I burn the piece of paper.

"Val Gule, what's happened?"

I look at Richard. "Get your army ready. We head for the

British water nation."

I walk out and Jay chases after me. "Is it Daniel? What's happened?"

I look at Jay, so angry that I can barely get the words out. "Members of his own army have made an attempt on his life."

Jay looks shell-shocked. "No, they wouldn't, surely."

I climb on my horse. "Tell her ladyship that."

He freezes on the spot and I ride over to Vision. "We found him, buddy, but he's injured we need to get to him quick. Find me the quickest route to Great Britain."

He takes off to do as I ask and I wait in anticipation. I'm angry. Very angry. I'm out for blood. Even if I have to burn down a thousand cities, I will get to him and I will take my revenge.

Jay

I can't believe it: members of his own army have made an attempt on his life.

I watch Dan Val Gule ride over to Vision and watch Vision fly off into the distance. I'm still not sure I believe him but when I think about it, Daniel does look a lot like him. I sit on the floor and curl up into a little ball. I keep telling myself he is going to be okay but in the back of my mind I am thinking of how I will find him when we get back to Britain. I'm thinking in my head how did they do it? Was it with fire? Was it with a weapon like a sword or a bow and arrow or did they just beat the shit out of him? Tears start to fall from my eyes imagining all of this.

I feel a nudge on my shoulder. I look round and see Valayrion, Richard's dragon. I turn to look at him. He licks my face, covering my face with saliva. Gorgeous, just what I wanted. He had good intentions though – he was probably trying to wipe my tears off my face. "What would you do in my situation?"

I shuffle over so that I can be under his wing and lean against his tummy. His wing moves closer to me as if he is cuddling me. He knows I am upset. I look up to see Richard.

"He likes you."

I give him a small smile as I am not in the mood to talk, let alone smile.

"Here." He throws a bag at me with some uniform in it. "It was mine. It should fit you; if not I'm sure we can find something else."

I pull out the uniform and it is the old fire nation uniform. It is bit worn because, of course, it has not only had a previous owner but it has probably been to battle several times. It is pretty similar to mine: black lose leggings with a black t-shirt and a wrap-up top with the fire nation symbol on the chest. On the top of the left sleeve are three red and yellow stripes which means co-general and four stripes mean general. He hands me some black boots which go half way up my shin and a cloak, black with fur going round the edge. The cloak is ridged, shaped like dragon scales. It only goes as far as your hips and you always only wear it on the plain side of your uniform so that the arm you are showing shows your rank.

I go to the nearest tent and put on the uniform, I feel a little bit like myself again. I place on these black leather gloves and make my way to Richard's tent.

"You look good. How does it feel to be in uniform again?"

I sigh. "Okay, but it's not quite my uniform. It carries someone else's achievements."

He shrugs and smiles. "I get, that but you needed it to show your rank. You will be back in your own uniform in no time."

Dan Val Gule enters. "I see you gave the boy your old uniform."

I roll my eyes. "Seriously! My name is Jay and I'm not a boy. I turned eighteen four years ago that makes me an adult."

He laughs. "You're a kid to me; I'm twice your age." He leans over Richard. "Vision did a flight and he reckons if we go this way we will be able to get to Daniel quicker."

I look at him, confused. "Or we can just go to the general of Finland and ask to borrow his plane?"

They both laugh. "Unfortunately, it is not that simple for us. Like you have said, we are wanted me. We will be arrested on the spot and they will arrest you for being with us, so we go under the radar."

I suppose they have a point. We don't really have a choice.

We pack up our tent, not that I have much to pack; it is literally only my clothes from when I was taken. I walk up to my horse and notice that Peter is saddling him.

"Hello."

He jumps and looks at me. "Hello, my lord, how are you?" He's shaking slightly.

"Feeling a bit shit, to be honest with you. How are you?"

He looks down and sheds a small tear. "Scared, to be honest, my lord. Is it true what they are saying about the general?"

I raise an eyebrow. I can tell he liked Daniel. "What are they saying?"

He finishes saddling my horse. "That he's the son of Dan Val Gule and the army tried to kill him?"

I sigh I can tell he's slightly upset about it. "One, I'm not so sure, to be honest and the other, yes, is true but either way he is still your general. He will still fight for you until his last breath. That's what the army is struggling to understand."

He smiles at me. "I'm not going to lie, my lord, it would be pretty awesome if he was Dan Val Gule's son." That just makes me dead confused. "Think about it – he will be the son of the most powerful fire manipulator in the world. That means that no matter what, we will always have Dan Val Gule and the Ripper on our side." He has a fair point.

"I'm your squire, by the way. The Ripper gave me that job."

I really don't need a squire but I will take it.

"You have a fair point. And awesome – at least it is someone I have met, I suppose." He smiles. He looks like a Peter, actually. "If you're lucky, Daniel might offer you a job when we get back."

He has so much hope in his eyes. "I would be honoured to serve him, my lord!" He's so cute. "He wouldn't want me, though – I'm not fit enough to do anything. I have always been a big guy."

I get up onto my horse and look at him. "Can you cook?" He nods. "There you go, there is your job: a chef. I will speak to Daniel when all is right with the world again."

He is so excited. "THANK YOU, MY LORD!"

I smile at him, I will speak to Daniel about that because he will be good to have around. "Just carry this stuff for me and I will see you shortly."

He smiles and goes to get onto his horse. Dan Val Gule comes up next to me. "Looks like you made someone's day."

I look at him. "Well, unlike you, I actually have a heart."

He laughs. "You don't think I have a heart?" I give him an evil glare. "You can give me that look all you want. If I didn't have a heart, you wouldn't be alive."

I still hate him. Until he tells Daniel his story and Daniel makes his decision, I will always hate him. All I want is for Daniel to be happy. He rides off.

"Don't test him. Whether you're Daniel's friend or not, he will kill you." I turn to see Richard riding up to me. "Regardless, he is getting his son back. He changed dramatically when he lost his son."

I looked at Richard. "I don't care. all I care about is Daniel. I'm still not convinced but I'm willing to let Daniel hear his story and decide for himself."

I start riding and Richard catches up with me. "Jay, he's dangerous and so is Daniel. If what you say about Daniel is true, he needs Dan Val Gule. He is the only one that can control his temper."

I look down with tears streaming down my face. "It's my fault this has happened, really."

He stops and looks at me dead in the eyes. "What do you mean?"

Now I am just scared. "Before I left to go undercover, a soldier warned me that some soldiers were saying some nasty shit about him. I should have told him but he was so quick at losing his temper – I must admit I was too scared." Richard looks at me with rage. "I told the water nation general to keep an eye on him but turns out the soldiers are better at planning than expected."

He gives me the angriest look known to man. "You best hope he doesn't find out," he says, pointing at Dan Val Gule, "otherwise you're dead."

I knew that would happen. "Then he would lose his son for good. You need to remember I'm like a brother to Daniel and he is stronger than he looks. If anyone touches me, he's out for blood and he will kill him."

Richard knows I am right and he rides away. I follow. I honestly can't wait to get home. If Daniel isn't awake, I know Valdamier will be there and I know he will have my back.

Gemma

I sit next to Daniel's bed just waiting. I feel his hands every day. They are cooling down and I don't know whether that is good or not. William also hasn't left his side ever since it happened. Apart from the Russians, he is the only fire manipulator I trust.

Dean walks in.

"Any sign of Jay yet?"

He shakes his head. I start to cry. The fire nation has attacked three times already. Thankfully, no lives have been lost.

Ivan walks in and I look at him. He looks at Dean and William. "Leave us."

They bow and walk out the room to stand outside. Ivan shuts the door. He slowly walks over to me, grabs a chair and sits next to me. "He is going to be okay, I know it." Ivan takes my hand.

"How can you be so sure?"

Valdameir walks in. "Because I have never known fire manipulators to be so stubborn."

I smile at him. They both embrace me with a hug.

"Valdameir, what can you tell me about Charles Knight?"

He freezes on the spot and Ivan stares at him. "How do you know about Charles Knight?"

I can see in his face that he is pissed off. "When I went to save Daniel, I overheard a bit of the conversation." He looks at me. "They said he was better than Daniel, that they want him back and he knows the purpose of the fire nation." He glares at me. "I know that you know something, Valdameir. I'm not stupid."

He walks to the other side of the bed. "It is best that you stay out of it."

Okay, now I'm angry. "NO, VALDAMEIR! I KNOW THAT YOU KNOW SOMETHING. WHAT AREN'T YOU TELLING ME?"

He turns round, absolutely raging. "HOW DARE YOU SPEAK TO ME LIKE THAT! YOU MAY BE GENERAL, YOUNG LADY, BUT I STILL RASIED YOU SO YOU WILL TREAT ME WITH RESPECT!" He walks so quickly over to me and comes so close to me I can feel his breath. "CHARLES KNIGHT WAS AN EVIL MAN. THAT IS ALL YOU NEED TO KNOW."

I glare at him. "YES, BUT HOW?"

He starts breathing heavily. "YOU ARE PUSHING MY BUTTONS, YOUNG LADY. THIS IS THE LAST I WANT TO HEAR OF THIS."

What is he so scared of? This is Valdameir – he is basically fearless. We continue to stare at each other then we hear a knock at the door.

"My lady, you have a visitor."

Valdameir looks at the door. "Stay here."

I storm out the door and look back at him. "I am a general, Valdameir, I'm not a little girl anymore."

Ivan walks up to me. "He's just trying to protect you, to be a father to you just as much as me."

I look at him with a saddened look then back at Valdameir with one that is just angry. "I know, and both of you are doing an amazing job but I need you both now more than ever."

Ivan nods and looks at Valdameir. "You're lucky I love you otherwise I would have told you to fuck off."

I smile at him and he smiles back. I regularly have arguments with Valdameir. He's probably the worst person to argue with but I still stand my ground because at the end of the day he was the one that taught me to do that.

I walk into the great hall and see a group of fire manipulators.

"My lady, my lords." He gives an evil grin.

"What do you want?"

He looks at Valdameir and my guards who are moving dangerously close to him. "It's obvious, isn't it? We want our general back to give him a proper send-off, you know?"

I glare at him.

"Oh please, my lady, you only shagged him once, that doesn't mean you own him. He belongs to us."

Valdameir looks at me in shock.

"You tried to kill him – what makes you think I would hand him over to you?"

He laughs and wipes a tear from his eye. "He's dead. I watched him fall to the floor."

I smiles so evilly, I can't help myself. "Oh, he's very much alive."

His eyes widen. "That's not possible; it should have killed him."

Valdameir moves in closer. "Attempting to kill your own general – you are all traitors and if I remember rightly, Phillip, you also took part in the wrong-doings of Charles Knight."

He looks at Valadmeir as he gives him a deadly look. "He knew what the fire nation stood for. Daniel is weak."

Valdameir laughs. "Charles Knight was an idiot. He put the whole fire nation at risk so I did what I had to do for the sake of the fire nation."

Phillip laughs. Ivan moves closer to me. "Oh please, how could he have done that?"

Valdameir smiles. "One name." He moveds closer to Phillip. "Dan Val Gule."

Phillip

He says that name and a shiver goes up my spine.

"Dan Val Gule, what does this have to do with him?"

He gives me an evil smile. "You will see, I'm sure. He is already on his way as her ladyship has contacted him and he won't be very happy."

I take a gulp. "Come on, boys."

We turn round and walk out the door. What the fuck does Dan Val Gule have anything to do with Daniel? We walk up the stony road to the fire nation house and I suddenly freeze. The other soldiers stop and look at me. "You guys go on, I have to take care of something." They nod and continue walking.

"You had one job, Phillip, one fucking job and you couldn't even pull that off". I take a massive gulp, knowing I am in a lot of trouble.

"You saw it, he was dead."

He makes an evil laugh as he comes out from the bushes behind me. "Didn't think to check?"

I am petrified. "We didn't have time; her ladyship turned up." I turn to look at him

"Yes, her ladyship interfered with our plan which doesn't surprise me." He moves closer to me.

"I take it you want me to kill her too?"

He smiles. "You are clearly as stupid as you look."

I raise an eyebrow. "What do you mean?" Why is it stupid? She's a woman – she's weak.

"I know what you're thinking. Just because she's a woman that makes her weak, right?"

I am confused. "Well, yeah. At least we can take the water nation now; that was the worst decision they ever made."

He shakes his head in disappointment. "No, it was the best decision they made and now she has had sex with Daniel she is ten times stronger than she already was, so you fucked up." He points at me.

"What are you talking about?"

He grins and walks up close to me. "This is all on you, Phillip. You wanted Jay back just as much as me."

I roll my eyes. "Only because he was fun."

He laughs and looks at me square in the eyes. He grips the back of my neck. "You will have to go in full-force. You have three days and you best hope in those three days Dan Val Gule doesn't arrive or Daniel doesn't wake up because otherwise it won't end very well." He looks at me with the most straight and emotionless face.

"Yes, my lord. We will attack in two."

He makes me kneel down in front of him. "Good." He grips my hair then comes down to my level. "Don't worry, I will give you one last chance. If Daniel is not dead, Jay is not in my possession and Gemma is not in my bed then we are going to have a small problem."

Gemma in his bed? "Oh, yes! She's beautiful, isn't she."

I take a gulp. He cups my testicles and squeezes them slightly. I squeal in pain. "Do I make myself clear?"

I nod. He lets go, gets up and wal off into the distance. I am breathing so heavily I start to feel dizzy. I sit on the floor for the moment hugging my knees. I have two days to prepare to take on the water nation. I best get started.

Gemma

After Phillip leaves, I decide to retire to my room. I am knackered and I don't have time for a lecture from Valdameir about me sleeping with Daniel.

I walk over to my wardrobe and rummage through my drawers to find something but I'm not satisfied. "I will sleep naked then."

I take off all my underwear and get into my duvet. Even though I am tired I can't sleep. I can't stop thinking about Daniel, what it felt like to be in his arms, what his touch felt like and his weird red eyes. As weird as it sounds, I found it quite sexy. I decide to get up and go into Daniel's room to lie next to him. I think I might sleep better if I am close to him.

I put on a thicker dressing gown because I am completely naked and walk down to his room. I nod at the guards outside and open the door. He is still passed out. I take off my dressing gown and lie under the covers next to him. I lie so close to him my breasts are touching his chest. I run my fingers around his scars, tracing every single one of them, visualising how he got each scar. I have so many questions in my head and no one is willing to answer them. I feel his hands and notice they are ice cold. Tears start streaming down my face.

"Please don't leave me." I start tracing one of the scars on his chest and move closer to him. I hold him in my arm and have my head on his chest. "Please."

I feel a hand touch the back of my head and start stroking

and playing with my hair. I look up and see Daniel's big brown eyes staring down at me. "Am I dreaming?" I sit up with my body on full display and cover my mouth with shock, still crying. "You're alive?"

He smiles at me and places his hand on my hip and stokes my tummy with his thumb. "Yeah, I guess I am."

I cry hysterically and fall onto him. He holds me so tight in his arms my whole body ends up on top of him. He kisses me on the head. I lift myself up to look at him. He stokes my cheek with his hand and pulls me in for a kiss. I can feel it growing underneath me. He sits up, still holding me. He stops kissing me and looks at me. "So beautiful." He grips my breast then kisses it.

The door flies open and Valdameir and Ivan come running in. I fly off of Daniel and hide my naked body under the covers.

"DANIEL!" They're so happy to see he is alive.

Valdameir looks at me and can see I am naked but doesn't say anything.

"How are you feeling?"

Daniel nods. "Yeah, okay."

Valdameir walks up to Daniel and hugs him while whispering something in his ear. I look at Ivan. Daniel looks at me then to Valdameir. What did Valdameir say?

Daniel

Fucking hell! I feel like I have been hit by a tank. My head is pounding. I open my eyes and see the water nation symbol in every corner of the room, although I am still seeing double.

I look down and see Gemma lying on my chest crying. Why is she crying? From what I can see she is completely naked. I can feel her breasts resting on my hips, her nice smooth skin up against my body. I move my hand and place it on the back of her head. I start playing with her long, gorgeous, silky smooth brown hair. She looks up at me. "Am I dreaming?" She sits up and the cover falls, leaving her beautiful body on full display. She is covering her mouth with tears streaming down her face. "You're alive?"

I place my hand on her hip and stroke her beautiful smooth skin with my thumb. "Yeah, I guess I am."

She starts to cry hysterically and falls on top of me. I hold her so tight. I don't want to let her go. I kiss her on the head then she looks at me and smiles. She straddles me. I hold her cheek in my hand and stroke it slightly. I pull her in for a kiss and place my hand on the bottom of her back. I slowly sit up as she places both of her hands on my cheeks. I have her wrapped in my arms and pulled he so close I can feel her vagina on my stomach. I stop the kiss and looked at her. "So beautiful." I grip her breast and gave it a little kiss then the doors fly open and Gemma flies off me.

Valdameir and Ivan come running through the doors. I look

directly at Valdameir and he looks furious.

"DANIEL!" At least Ivan is happy to see me. "How are you feeling?"

I nod at him. "Yeah, okay." I'm not. I am feeling rough and now, thanks to Gemma, very horny. Valdameir walks up to me and hugs me. He starts whispering something in my ear.

"Daniel, if you're not careful you will kill her. She may have survived once but how many times is it going to take you before she dies?"

I look a Valdameir and then to Gemma. She looks at me, intrigued by what was said.

"Shower and eat. You will feel better." I nod at Ivan as he orders for some food and a glass of water to be brought up here. "We will talk about this later, young lady," he warns Gemma.

Food is brought up to the room with a glass of water; a full English breakfast, my favourite.

"So what news is there?"

Valdameir sits forwards in his chair. "Not much. We know that Phillip is behind the attack but he can't be working alone – he doesn't have the balls for that." I look at Valdameir, scared to death of what he is going to say next. "Still no sign of Jay, either."

I down my water and slam my fork into my bacon. "Right, okay. Have you got any leads?" I look to Gemma.

"Not yet. Whoever took him is good at going off the grid, so it could be anyone."

I finish my breakfast and the soldiers take it away from me. "Well, I'm here now so I can help where I can."

Ivan laughs. "You're still going to be a bit too weak; you need to rest." Valdameir and Ivan get up. "Shower, Daniel; you will feel better."

They leave the room. Gemma has to stay in the bed until they are all gone then she gets up and puts her dressing gown on.

"Where you off to?"

She smiles. "Ivan's right, you need to rest."

She walks over to my side of the bed and kisses me on the lips. "Get some rest."

I grab her hand and pull her back to me. I sit on the edge of the bed and pull her in front of me. "I have had enough rest, don't you think?"

She smiles at me. I untie her dressing gown, revealing her naked body. She places her hand on my shoulder. I run my hands up her legs, round her hips, up her stomach to her breasts. I give them a little massage then run my hands down her back and place one hand on each ass cheek. I look up at her as she is watching me feel every inch of her body. I kiss the bottom of the tummy then make my way down to her vagina.

"Oh, yes!" I start to just kiss her then I taste her. I put my tongue in. "Oh, yes!" She grips my hair on the back of my head. "Ah, Daniel!" I move my hands up her body to grip her breasts. "Oh Daniel, please don't stop!" I don't plan, to not until I have tasted her. Her legs start shaking and I stop. I kiss up her body and slowly stand up.

"Fancy joining me in the shower?" She looks at me, worn out and confused. I pull her close to me. "Trust me."

She smiles and I walk her to the bathroom. She goes in first to turn on the shower. As she is checking the temperature, I couldn't stop myself, I wrap my arms around her, taking both breasts in my hands and pulling her close.

"Hey, the water's not ready."

I laugh and kiss her on the neck. I make my way down to her vagina and start to tease her. "Oh Daniel, that's not fair."

I smile and continue to tease her. She gets her own back. She leans in to check the water, making sure that her ass is touching my penis. I am so tempted just to put it in but that isn't the way I work. She turns around and looks down. Her eyes look back up to me and she grins. "Water's ready."

She reaches down and has a little play. I bite my lip. I hold her close as I lead her into the shower. We get under the square shower head and start to make out. She wraps her arms around my neck and I pull her so close to me that we could become one.

I make sure her whole body is wet then I move her back to the wall. I have her so tight against it she isn't going anywhere. Her eyes go from a beautiful brown to an icy blue. Interesting. I kiss her on the neck, move my hand down and place my fingers inside.

"Oh Daniel!"

That's right, say my name. I stick them so far up that her moans get louder. I feel so much power go through me I have to do it, I have to do it now. I pick her up and she wraps her legs around my hips. I hold both of her arms against the wall and thrust my penis into her.

"Ah!" This time I can't stop. "Yes Daniel, yes, harder!"

I thrust as hard and as fast as I can. My fists start to light up with fire, making me go faster. She forces her way out of my hands and wraps her arms around my neck. "Keep going!" She is close to a massive orgasm. I kiss her on the neck. The fire slowly makes its way down my arms. "AH YES! YES!" I accidentally touch her breasts but I don't burn her.

"Oh Gemma!" I start to slow down as I completely orgasm inside her. I pull out and catch her before she falls to the floor. I pick her up and take her to the bed and tuck her in. I go back into the bathroom to wash my body and my hair then turn it off. I walk back out to the bedroom and see her asleep in bed. I dry myself off and climb in the bed next to her and take her in my arms.

What the fuck was that? That has never happened before. That if Valdameir's right? Could I have killed her tonight? And more importantly, her eyes turned blue? That is definitely not normal.

Jay

The ride to Daniel is long and tiring but it is worth it. We have already stopped for rest twice but Dan Val Gule is so determined we don't stop for very long. I take out my dragon figure that I bought and it is now fully awake with its wings spread apart. Like I said, I could have sworn it was sleeping.

Finding out about Daniel's potential past was heart-breaking but at least he possibly has someone now. It is making me question my whole life, though. I literally remember nothing about my past, like where I came from or who my parents are.

"I know that look." Richard has stopped and waited for me.

"What look?"

He smiles. "The 'contemplating life' look. Elijah use to catch me doing it all the time."

Elijah laughs. "Yep, he was dreadful at it."

I make a small smile. "Just tired, that's all."

He smiles and shakes his head. "You're thinking about your past." I look at him, slightly shocked. "Relax, it's normal. You have just found out about Daniel and now you want to know about yourself." I look back down at the figure in my hand and come to a halt. Richard comes up in front of me. "Look, I know you want to know more about yourself and someday I'm sure you will but sometimes things are better left unknown." I look at him, confused. What does he know about me that I don't? "You feel lost, alone, second best and scared." He pretty much nailed it.

"I don't even know who I am, to be honest. I'm struggling."

I feel like I can open up to Richard a little. I feel like he knows how I feel.

"Trust me, I know how you feel. I was third best because I have two brothers. My father hates my guts; my brother gets everything and I get nothing." He is basically me.

"When was the last time you saw your father?"

He sniggers. "When I was about fifteen. He tortured me. Loved my brothers, but hated me and I never knew why."

I roll my eyes. "I know how you feel. The amount of torture I went through with the previous general, I could have jumped off a cliff at any point but I didn't. I kept going because I had Daniel, but I still felt alone."

He smiles. "It won't be forever, trust me." I sure hope not.

"RICHARD!" Dan Val Gule is never quiet, I swear.

We ride up to the front where he is and sees a camp. "A wanna-be army."

As I look closer, I can see in the distance three soldiers wearing their uniform.

"They have ships too," Richard points out.

"Charge!"

The army charges down and overloads the camp, tearing down tents, removing heads, you name it. When the slaughter is over, we ride down to the camp and I see that the three soldiers are being held up for questioning but none of them are answering.

"You all have balls, I will give you that." I walk closer to them and Dan Val Gule stands to the side of me. "You two are British and you, my friend, are Russian." Oh dear, he's brown bread.

"A Russian?" I look at Richard.

"Yep, his uniform is slightly different; it has the Russian flag on the top of their left sleeve. Theirs has the British flag."

I grin at him. "I can't wait for Valdameir to come face to face with you." I look at Dan Val Gule; he is smiling. "Do we take prisoners?"

He shakes his head. "But in this case, for the same reason as you, from what I have heard about this Valdameir, I'm taking him prisoner." The soldiers chain him up. "But what to do with you two. Do we take you back to Daniel or do I just crack on with it now?" One of them I recognise immediately. "In fact, I think I know someone who will take great pleasure in killing you, but first you're going to answer a few questions."

I walked up close to him.

"You don't scare me, Jay."

I laugh at him. "Ha, you might regret that."

He laughs. "Really, and what are you going to do to me?"

Valayrion lands behind me. "You know, you should never judge a book by its cover, or did they not teach you that in bellend school?" Richard is grinning so hard that his face will start hurting soon. "Why? What has Daniel ever done to you?"

Vision lands to the side of me as soon as he hears Daniel's name. "He's weak; he knows nothing about the fire nation or its purpose."

Dan Val Gule laughs. "And what purpose is that exactly?"

He looks at him. "Pride, glory, royalty and fear."

Richard cries with laughter as well as members of the army. Dan Val Gule raises an eyebrow and looks at me. "Because just like everyone else around me, including me, Daniel thought it was a load of bollocks."

I feel so much power right now. "Dan Val Gule, I have a present for you." He looks at me. "This is Jason, one of Daniel's abusers." I walk over to the other soldier. "Watch and learn what happens when you pick on the fire nation general."

Dan Val Gule is furious.

"I'm not scared of you."

He makes an evil laugh. "Hear that, boys? He's not scared of me!" They all crack up laughing. "You should be." He walks up to Vision. "This is Vision. He's been a bit upset lately because my son went missing eighteen years ago." He looks at Richard. "Notice how he looks a bit happier, Richard?"

Richard grins. "Oh yes, he does look very happy."

He walks up to Jason. "That's because we have finally found my son." Jason can't take his eyes off Vision. "Want to know who that is?" He is now looking at Dan Val Gule. "Daniel. So, your general."

Jason gulps. "Well, he's dead, so what a shame."

Vision looks at Dan Val Gule. "Ha. He's not dead, son, he is very much alive." He looks back at Vision.

"Vision seems bit hungry, Val Gule, I think he could do with a snack."

I grin. "Do you know what, I think Valayrion looks bit hungry too, what do you two reckon?"

They both smile at me. "Go on, boys, have a spot of lunch."

Dan Val Gule gives Jason to Vision and I give the other soldier to Valayrion. They both set them on fire first and then they grab their bodies in their mouths and at them whole. I stand there and watch as Valayrion eats one of my abusers; it is the most satisfying moments of my life. It sounds bad but I am getting my revenge. The power I felt the moment Valayrion landed behind me, I knew I had them in the palm of my hands.

Richard

After that interesting turn of events we board the ships and I go straight to one of the offices. I look inside and it is pretty basic. It has a small desk in the middle with two small chairs, one either side, and just a few empty shelves.

I grab all my paperwork and sit on one of the chairs and started going through it all. I hear a knock at the door then Dan Val Gule walks in.

"You never give me time to say come in." I grin.

He laughs at me then sits in the chair opposite. "You know me, I don't wait."

I shrug in agreement. "Where's our little tag-along?"

He smiles. "Passed out on one of the beds; he was a tired boy." I pour him a drink and push it over to him. "I do have a question though."

I sit there intrigued. "What's that?" He never comes to see me just because he wants to; there is always a reason.

"Did you ever have a son?"

Well, that is a bit of a sore subject.t "I would rather not talk about that. You know I don't like that topic of conversation."

He rolls his eyes. "I just wondered because Jay is basically a mini you. Valayrion loves him and you both get on really well."

I laugh a little. "So you think he's my son because he is funny and Valayrion likes him?"

He gives me a straight look. "No, not funny. He acts like a twat. And yes, Valayrion loves him."

I refill my drink. I don't really know how to take that. "Well, he's not and I know he's not."

He looks at me and laughs. "He must be. Maybe you accidentally got a girl pregnant and she got scared so she handed him to the general."

I give him the most serious look I can. "I'm telling you, he is not my son."

He rolls his eyes and stands up. He places his hands on his hips. "I'm trying to give you hope here. I know how much you wanted a son."

I walk over to the window and watch the water underneath the boat. "I can't have children, Val Gule, even if I wanted to."

He walks over to me. "What? Of course you can. If someone like me can have a son, so can you! You're a much better person than I am. I'm an evil bastard, never deserved a son, but I got one."

He really isn't getting the message and once again it's all about him. "Val Gule, I mean it, I can't, and once again it's all about you. Honestly, what is it with you. You can never feel sorry for someone without making your life sound worse."

He laughs. "Why are you so against it? And I don't make everything about myself."

Oh dear god, Dan Val Gule is powerful and wise but he isn't very smart. "I don't have any testicles so I will never be able to produce children."

He looks at me in complete shock. "What? How?"

A tear streams down my face. "Our dad had them surgically removed when I was younger. I haven't had them for basically my whole life. It was so I don't reproduce; he hated me that much."

He launches a glass across the room and it smashes into a

million little pieces. "WHY DIDNT YOU TELL ME!"

I just stand there. He is angry, yes but I don't give a shit. "You never noticed how bad of a father he was because you were too busy fighting with Vang-Chi."

He punches the wall, leaving a dent in the steel. "I would have killed him, Richard. We ran away because of how horrible he was being to you, all three of us, and you told neither of us!"

This is where he will lose it. "That's not strictly true." I can feel his rage from where I am standing.

"You told Vang Chi but not me?"

I nod.

"WHY?"

Now I am getting angry. "WHY SHOULD I? YOU NEVER CARED ABOUT ME OR WHAT I WANTED. IT WAS ALL ABOUT YOU!"

He leans against the desk, trying to control his anger. "I cared about you, Richard, and I always will. Why do you think I haven't killed Jay?"

I laugh and stare out the window. "Because he's Daniel's best friend."

He does a small laugh. "No, you fucking idiot, because of you!"

I look at him in shock. "Jay comes from nowhere, he has no family, he is exactly like you, thinks the whole world is against him all the time."

Okay, that last part makes me livid. He sits down on the chair. "THE WHOLE WORLD IS AGAINST ME, VAL GULE! I LOVED SOMEONE ONCE AND SHE WAS KILLED. SHE WAS FIFTEEN, VAL GULE, FUCKING FIFTEEN! SHE DIED BECAUSE SHE LOVED ME, SO STOP ACTING LIKE YOU CARE. AT LEAST VANG CHI WAS THERE FOR ME WHEN

IT HAPPENED." I fall to my knees and try to picture her in my head.

"I'm sorry, Richard."

Jay suddenly walks through the door. "Yo, I know you guys are brothers 'n' all but I'm trying to sleep and all I can hear is shouting and screaming and not in a good way." He registers that I am on the floor crying. "What's happened?"

He walks over to me and looks at Dan Val Gule. "Tell him, Richard."

I get up and look at Dan Val Gule. "The only reason me and you stayed in contact was for Daniel – because I couldn't have that." I look at Jay. "See me now? See what I mean? You think you've got it hard."

I walk out the room and decide to go to one of the bedrooms. I pull out a picture of Marie. I miss her every single day. I love you, Marie.

Gemma

I lie next to Daniel, looking at him while he sleeps. He turns round, puts his arms around me and pulls me closer. I bury my head in his chest and take in all his smell.

"Good morning, beautiful."

I look up and he smiles at me as he is slowly waking up.

"Good morning, handsome."

He kisses me on the forehead, pulls me in even closer so that our bodies are touching. He strokes my cheek and tucks my hair behind my ear then moves for a kiss. He pulls me on top of him.

"Ah!" He inserts his penis inside me I lean down to kiss him. He grips hold of my breasts and we start to make out as he thrusts as hard as he can.

Bells start ringing. I stop kissing him and climb off him. "Shit!"

I run out hi room to mine and quickly put on my battle gear. Unfortunately, it is a long dress with the water nation symbol on the side, waist armour which covers everything and my armoured waist bands. I walk out the room and meet Valdameir and Ivan in the great hall with Mikhill and Frank.

"So, how far away are they?"

We start walking to the battle grounds where all three armies have assembled.

"Minutes away."

I walk to the front of my army and climb on my horse; Valdameir and Ivan do the same. We wait in anticipation for the army to arrive. As we are waiting, a massive line of fire is produced and a load of fire manipulators that I have never seen before come charging at us.

"Archers!" All the archers came forth. "To the ready!" They load up their bows with arrows. "Take your aim!" I wait a few seconds. "Fire!" They release probably about a hundred arrows. I watch them fly through the air. Just as they're about to hit, I call, "Charge!"

Me, Ivan and Valdameir crash into our opponent. I stand on the back of my horse and flip off while removing the swords from their sleeves and slicing two soldiers' throats open. I slowly move them in front of me, making a cross to produce an ice wall then move them apart quickly to make the wall longer. I place my swords back in their sleeves, place my hands down by my hips and stretch them out so far, a massive radiation wave of power shatter it, turning it into spears of ice so sharp they can pierce a living being. I start looking at certain fire manipulators who are targeting my men and fire all my spears at them.

I am then surrounded by my opponents. One of them kicks me so hard I fly a few feet. I hold my stomach as it hurt so much. They all walk over to me and grin. I hold my stomach once more. I can hardly breathe; for some reason the kick has really knocked me back. In Russia, I used to be able to take a kick like that but for some reason I feel weak. I am down permanently.

"MY LADY!"

I suddenly feel hot and notice that I am surrounded by fire. Daniel walks next to me. His eyes are on fire, his arms are on fire, everything. He stands in front of me and raises his arms. He lets out a roar like a dragon and the ring of fire grows, covering us completely. His body is so hot all of his clothes burn off him. He raises his arms above his head and creates a curricular movement with his hands and half of the circle is transformed into a rather large dragon. It is amazing and terrifying at the same time.

I can see in the gap my army has fallen back along with Valdameir's and Ivan's. Daniel swiftly moves the hands from the top of his head and the dragon starts to fly over the soldiers of the enemy, frying all of them alive until they are ashes.

"FALL BACK! FALL BACK NOW!" I hear the enemy say.

The dragon comes back to Daniel and he turns to me. He kneels down next to me with his eyes and his body still on fire. He places his hand on my stomach and kisses me on the forehead then collapses; the fire disappears from around me and I just lie there.

"GEMMA!" Valdameir and Ivan run up to me as I sit up. "Are you okay?"

I look round me and notice that I am covered in ashes and the whole field is burning.

"Daniel?" Valdameir checks for a pulse. "OUCH!" I look at him. "He must be recharging or something."

I laugh. Ivan picks me up. "Come on, let Valdameir deal will Daniel. Let's get you cleaned up and put to bed." I cuddle up to him as he carries me to my room. Galina follows us and runs me a bath.

"It's okay, Ivan, I have got it from here."

He nods. "I will be on the battle grounds helping clear up and doing a count if I can." He rolls his eyes and then gives me a kiss on the forehead.

I sit on the toilet in pure silence as Galina runs me a bath. She helps me get in and starts washing my body. I can't stop thinking about what I just saw.

"Are you okay, my darling?" I look at Galina, still shaking.

"It was your first proper fight darling, it would always shake you up."

It wasn't that. "It was Daniel's eyes, Galina. They were pure fire, like you couldn't see his eyeballs. It was awesome but terrifying."

She washes my hair for me. I love it when Galina washes my hair; she always gives it a good scrub.

"I'm going to have to get Ivan or Valdameir to lift you out." We wait for the water to go down then Galina gives me a towel to cover myself with. "Valdameir is coming. I'm just going to dry you off and get you some clothes."

I nod at her she gets me my favourite large jumper and a comfortable pair of knickers to put on. I still felt too weak to even move. Valdameir knocks on the door and walks in.

"Come on then, trouble." He picks me up and carries me out to my bed. Galina pulls back my covers and he places me in bed, just like old times. He sits on the edge of the bed and tucks my hair behind my ear. "Before you ask, Daniel is fine, just very tired."

I smile at him. "Valdameir, can you tell me a story like you used to?"

Galina sits on the other side of the bed and Ivan walks in and sits next to her.

"Once upon a time, there was this beautiful young girl. No one knew her background. No one knew who she was or what she was capable of." Water maipulators from my army and Ivan's army come into the room, along with Valdameir's army. "She grew up stronger and grew more beautiful every day." Some of the army sit down listening to the story. "She was raised in Russia by three very important people." He takes my hand. "The water nation general, the fire nation general and his wife." I lie there looking at him listening to his story.

"One day, she was told that she would be the next general of the Great British water nation. Yes, she wasn't happy about it but she took the position with honour." He looks round at the army. "Her men took her under their wing and she grew to be their general. She loved every single one of them." He smiled. "But one day she fell victim to a forbidden love with the British fire nation general." My smile fades.

He lets go of my hand and stokes my hair. "It was not her fault or his fault, as no one can help who they do and don't love. When the fire nation general who raised her found out, he was furious! All he wanted to do was rip him to pieces but he didn't want to lose her so he warned the boy that if he hurt her, he would kill him." He smiles at me I laugh a little. "He wanted to support her in any way he could." He sits closer to me and I lift my head up and place it on his lap as tears start to leave my eyes.

"This young lady had to save her dear love's life and war came to her door step. Was she ready for it? No. Was she scared? Of course." He stokes my hair as I cry. "But she did it anyway and those men she led into battle followed her, even the ones that didn't believe in her at first, but they saw her potential that night."

I wipe my tears off my face. "What's the story called?" I sit up and rested my head on his shoulder.

"The complicated life of the warrior princess."

I cry and laugh at the same time. I hug him so tight. "Why is my life so complicated?"

He cradles me in his arms. "Because you're stronger than you think. You just need to embrace it. We all believe in you."

I look at him. "Will you stay with me like you did when I was a little girl?"

He smiles and nods. Valdameir, Ivan and Galina stay with me while Frank makes sure there are at least five people outside my door. I fall asleep feeling like I am at home again.

Dan Val Gule

We finally arrive at the water nation boarder. I want to see Daniel but I can't stop thinking about Richard and what our father did to him. I feel guilty that I have everything that he wants. It isn't fair on him.

"Val Gule, you need to see this!" Richard leads me to the front of the ship and what I see is just phenomenal: a massive dragon made purely out of fire.

I stand next to Jay as he watches with his mouth wide open. "Is that normal?"

This massive wall of fire which I assume is surrounding him is so tall; only a very, very powerful fire manipulator could create such a thing. "I think we have definitely found him, Val Gule."

I nod still in shock from what I am seeing, but I can't help but feel proud because that is my son right there. I have never been able to produce a dragon that large out of fire. He is definitely a lot more powerful than me, maybe even a lot more powerful than my brother and father. To be honest, that scares me.

I look at Richard, concerned. He stares the same look. "This is going to be tough."

Richard nods. "Worse comes to worst, Val Gule, we will try and find Vang Chi, but I'm sure it will be fine." I really don't want to have to call on him to help me with my son.

We finally reach land. "I should probably go first." Jay has a point so I nod. Almost half an army of water nation soldiers are guarding the borders.

"My lord!"

Jay walks off the ship and approaches the nearest soldier.

"Is her ladyship here?"

He smiles. "She is, but I will have to get Ivan. She is unwell."

One of the other soldiers sniggers. "More like traumatised. She was right in the middle of that." One of them goes off to find Ivan. Poor girl was right in the middle of it? I'm not surprised she is traumatised.

Ivan makes his way through the crowd. "Jay, it's about time." He smiles and gives Jay a hug.

"I brought a few guests with me."

Ivan looks at me and Richard then looks at Jay. "I noticed."

I walk up to him. "Dan Val Gule." I put out my hand and he shakes it.

"Ivan, the water nation general of Russia."

I nod. "Looks like we missed a good fight."

He smiles. "Well, you missed more than that." He motions us to follow. "I will have to take you to Valdameir first. I believe he has a few rules for you because at the moment you can't be trusted, for obvious reasons."

I understand that Valdameir is only being cautious. I look round and the gardens have been completely destroyed. I can imagine it was quite beautiful once.

They all start running in different directions as Vision and Valayrion land in the gardens. Ivan looks at me and Richard. "That's one way to piss Valdameir off."

Richard and I smile. We walk into the great hall which is rather big and rather beautiful. "Wait here."

Jay looks around. "Last time I was here I got absolutely battered." Richard smiles at him. He is definitely more and more like him every day.

Finally, Valdameir comes out of the hallway on the right-hand side of the great hall. "Ah Jay! It's good to see you again, my friend!" He embraces Jay with a hug.

"How is he?"

Valdameir looks at Jay with a worried face. "Completely passed out but he's alive. But Gemma is my main concern at the moment."

Richard steps forwards and speaks first. "What happened?"

Valdameir approaches us. "I couldn't even explain it even if I wanted to. The best person for you to talk to is Gemma but she is resting at the moment." Understandable.

"Can we see him?" Back to my primary concern.

"Yes, but I have a few rules: you will not go into either Daniel's or Gemma's room without me or Ivan; you let us know where you are going at all times so we can keep an eye on you; and above all, control those bloody dragons."

Richard and I smile and nod. He leads us down the hallway and I walk in o a rather decently sized room and lying in the bed is Daniel. "How long has he been like this?"

I look at Valdameir. "Roughly a day. He passed out as soon as the wall of fire vanished."

I feel his head. "He will only be out for a few more hours." Valdameir nods. "What about her ladyship? How is she doing?"

He looks at me then looks at Daniel. You can tell he is angry. "She is getting worse." That shocks me; usually water manipulators recover quickly.

"May we see her? We might be able to help," Richard asks. It was a good idea – she might be able to tell me what's going on. Valdameir nods and leads us to Gemma's room. He knocks on the door.

"Who is it?"

Valdameir smiles. "Your husband, my love."

I look at Richard, dead confused. "Come in." We open the door and she is nowhere to be seen. "Bear with us; she has just thrown up."

Is it really that bad? Is she really that traumatised?

Valdameir helps her back into bed. She does not look well at all. I walk over to her side of the bed and take a seat. I take her hand. "I'm Dan Val Gule, my lady." I kiss her hand.

"Hello." I look at the poor girl and really do feel sorry for her.

"Tell me, what happened?"

Water nation soldiers flood the room. They are obviously over-protective of her.

"His eyes – they were flames. His whole body was lit up on fire. He produced a dragon with only half of the fire he had already made, the other half was surrounding us." Her eyes widen. "Galina!"

She grabs a bowl quick and Gemma throws her guts up. I hold her hand and watch as she has her head over the bowl. "It's okay, dear, get it all out." She sits up and nods at Galina.

She looks at me again. "It didn't stop there. He turned to me; I thought he was going to kill me. He knelt down next to me, placed his hand on my stomach and kissed me on the forehead, then he collapsed."

I look at her in complete shock. "Elderflower tea, that should stop the sickness and make her feel a little bit more like herself." I get up and pace the room. "Have you had sex with Daniel?"

She looks at me, confused. "Yes."

Valdameir realises where I am going with this. "Val Gule, how the fuck is she still alive?"

I shake my head. "I don't know, but we have a very, very big problem. I need to speak to him as soon as he wakes up." I look at Richard. "Find him."

Richard nods. Now I know I can't do this alone. What she has described is beyond my power and knowledge. I look up at Valdameir. "By the way, we have a present for you."

I walk out the door and he follows me to the great hall.

Valdameir

I walk into the great hall behind Dan Val Gule and see a member of my army in chains with Jay stood behind him.

"What is this? Why is a member of my army in chains?"

Jay looks at me and smiles. "Well, go on, tell him why you are in chains." The soldier remains quiet.

"Jay, what is going on?"

Jay rolls his eyes and walks close to me. "He's betrayed you, Valdameir. He was in the enemy's camp working for them."

I give the soldier the dirtiest look I can. "Is this true?" The soldier is shaking; he doesn't say a word. "SPEAK!"

He gulps and finally looks at me. He is only young, I would say twenty-eight, if that, with blonde hair, green eyes, and quite a small build. I do remember him; he is a very big-headed lad. I have been keeping my eye on him for a while.

"He is right, my lord, I have betrayed you."

I am beyond furious. Mikhail places his hand on my shoulder and whispers in my ear, "My lord, remember he is only young."

I turn to him. "What are you saying exactly?" He knows I don't take it lightly when someone betrays me.

"Find out the full story then make your decision." He is right, I suppose.

"Well, why betray me? Have I treated you poorly?" He shakes his head. "Then why?"

He gives me an angry look. He looks at Mikhail then his eyes direct back to me. "You're the traitor, Valdameir."

Jay laughs. "I will give it to him, he's brave."

My eyes widen. I look at a few members of my army; all of them looked confused. "How is that, exactly?"

He laughs and shakes his head. "You raised a water manipulator. You're a fucking fire manipulator! Charles Knight is right, you are weak. You know nothing, Valdameir. I stopped fighting for you a long time ago because I questioned who you were actually fighting for – the fire nation or the water nation."

My army starts whispering. "All it takes is for your army to turn against you and you're fucked."

Then they all crack up laughing. I grin. "ARE YOU NUTS!" They all continue to laugh. "My lord, we know he's young but are you going to take that?"

I look at Mikhail and smile. He smiles back, knowing that I won't. "Yes, I raised a water manipulator, no I don't fight for the water nation, I fight for her – there is a slight difference – and yes I do know everything, as do the men in my army, those that are wise anyway." I walk up closer to him. "Charles Knight is not right; he doesn't know the meaning of the fire nation. If I were replaced, the Russian fire nation would fall and all respect would be lost." I look at my captain Viktor (long black shoulder length hair, dark skinned, tall and muscular) and he grins at me. "Take him to the centre of the army." He picks him up and walks him out. "Mikhail, get my sword." He smiles.

"Jay, you look very excited." Jay is literally shaking with excitement.

"I've never seen you execute anyone." I grin and motion him to follow. Viktor has him kneeled down in front of Gemma's army and my army. Dan Val Gule follows, intrigued.

"My lord, please."

I laugh. I look up to see Galina. I walk up to her and stroke her cheek. "Darling, you should not be watching."

She takes her hand in mine. "He called you a traitor; I want to watch him pay."

I kiss her on the forehead and turn to the soldier. "What's your name?" He looks up at me, crying. "QUIT CRYING AND TELL ME YOUR NAME!"

He looks to another soldier, who raises an eyebrow. I look to him and notice he is crying. "Dad, please." I continue to look at him.

"Why, Lev?" I feel sorry for him, but he betrayed me.

I approach him. "You understand why I have to do this?" He nods. The soldier next to him places his arm around him. "Make sure he is comforted; he is losing a son today." He nods.

"Remove his top." The soldiers remove his top. I heat up my hand. I place my hand on his stomach. He screams in pain. "This burn is for betraying your general." I remove my hand then place my hand on his back. "This burn is for accusing your general of betrayal." I come up in front of him and place my hand on his heart and start to melt his skin. "This is for breaking your father's heart." I notice Galina approach his father and take him in her arms. "I, Valdameir, general of the Russian fire nation, sentence you, Lev, to Death." I take a deep breath and plunge my sword through his stomach, swiftly turn it then remove it. Blood comes pouring out his mouth. My soldiers move. I hand my sword over to Mikhail and open my palms. A massive ball of fire comes pouring out. I don't stop until he is ashes. Galina walks up behind me. I look at her with tears in my eyes. "It had to be done, my love." I take her in my arms and slowly start to cry. If there is one thing I hate doing its killing members of my army. I walk up to his father. "I am sorry, but I did not have a choice."

He nods then looks at me, his eyes swollen. "I know, my

lord." I place my hand on his shoulder and pull him in for a hug. "I am sorry for what he did."

I pull away and place my hand on his cheek. "He was led down the wrong path. I will pray to the dragon spirt that he sees that before making the decision." He smiles. "You may collect up his ashes and give him a good send-off when we get home."

One of the other soldiers brings up a pot and they all help him collect his ashes. Viktor approaches me. "Are you okay, my lord? I know how much you hate doing that." I shake my head.

"To be honest, Viktor, no I'm not. I hated every minute of it." I watch as they all help Lev's father. Galina even chips in. "It was his father I felt sorry for. No father should have to bury their child and every time I do it I feel like I have failed."

Viktor shakes his head. "No, my lord, you haven't, not by a long shot." He sighs. "You are probably the best general we have had. Like you said, the boy was lead down the wrong path. At least you gave his father the chance to give his son a proper send-off." I nod.

A man I do not recognise comes up next to me. I know who he is immediately. "To what do I owe this honour?"

He gives that warm fatherly smile. He is an old man, with scruffy white hair, trousers that are too short for him and a checked top. "You know who I am, don't you, Valdameir?"

I nod. "Did I do the right thing?"

He nods. "Absolutely. He betrayed his general. I know you feel sorry for the father and as his general, you would, but sometimes you have to put duty before love." I grin and look at him. "You're a wise man, Valdameir. Russia would be lost without you. I will consider what you have said, I promise." I bow to him as he walks off into the distance. I feel like a terrible general but I know I have to sometimes put duty before love.

Daniel

I wake up with the biggest headache known to man, probably worse than the one the last time I woke up. My whole body is aching, head to toe. I slowly sit myself up and start to heavily breathe as that in itself takes all the effort from me. I cover my face with my hands, which I have noticed are boiling hot, and rub my eyes. I look in front of me and see a male figure sitting at the end of my bed with his legs crossed. As my vision adjusts, I can see him a little more.

"It's about fucking time!"

I have never felt more relieved and happy in my life to hear that voice. My vision fully adjusts and I see Jay sat there grinning at me. "You took your time. I was starting to age a bit here."

I laugh at him then he lean in for a hug. "Good to see ya, man." He is never leaving my side again.

"It's good to see you, too." He sits back down. "So, is there something you've got to tell me?"

I don't think he could grin any wider. "Like what? I have been in this bed for most of the time you have been gone."

He cracks up laughing. "You know what I mean." He moves over to sit next to me with his legs laid out. "So how did it happen?"

Oh, now I know what he's talking about. "That's private."

He laughs. "Nothing between me and you is private. Now come on, tell me! Was it good?" I'm not going to lie. I have missed him.

"Best sex I have ever had."

He fist-bumps me and laughs. "Well, it was about time. I was getting bit bored of the new Daniel." Ouch, that hurts a bit.

"Yet you would never leave me."

He lets out a little laugh. "Well you're going to need me now more than ever."

I raise an eyebrow, confused, and in walks Dan Val Gule. I jump out of my bed, quickly notice that I am fully naked, and grab a towel from the bathroom to wrap round my bottom half.

"Jay, what the fuck is he doing here?"

Jay looks far too relaxed for my liking. "Relax, he's not here to kill you." I stand to my side, ready to attack.

"Unclench those fists, boy, I'm not going to hurt you." I feel so angry I can't control it; they start to light up. "You can't control your power, I see."

Galina walks in behind him and looks at me, shocked and angry. "YOU BEST UNCLENCH THOSE FISTS YOUNG MAN OR I WILL BE FORCED TO GET MY HUSBAND."

I can't cope with another lecture from Valdameir. I unclench my fists and Dan Val Gule looks at Galina with a curious face.

"Get out, all of you. The boy needs to shower and change! Jay, you may stay if you wish."

He laughs. "Well, I have definitely seen it all now and I'm comfy, so I will stay."

She throws some clothes at me and points to the bathroom. "Shower, now!"

She's very angry about something, which makes me think that Valdameir is probably even worse. I step into the shower and reimagine my time with Gemma, how close I was to killing her. I can't do that too her again. We have to stop, but I can't; she's like a drug, she's an addiction. I can still feel her soft skin against mine, not forgetting those icy blue eyes – that was just weird. I can hear Galina and Jay in the next room having a little argument. "Oh please, he's allowed to have sex." I knew it was about that.

"He could have killed her! Not to mention the trauma she went through!" What the hell is she talking about?

"Don't worry, Gemma will be fine; she is stronger than she looks!" I get out the shower and stand by the door.

"I know she is, I raised her, remember? Thanks to Dan Val Gule, she is improving. Who knew it was something as simple as elderflower tea?" I can't. I need answers.

I walk out the room with a towel wrapped round my waist. "I almost killed her, didn't I?" I look at Galina with tears in my eyes.

"No, you didn't. She is still alive just poorly." Galina looks at Jay, furious. "Valdameir will be in shortly; he is getting an update on Gemma now." She walks out the door after changing my bed. I sit there staring at the floor.

"Even with all that power in your palms, you're still scared of Valdameir?"

I look at Jay. "I respect him. He saved our skins; if it wasn't for him, we probably wouldn't be here. We owe him our lives, Jay." He comes over and sits next to me. "Why is he here?"

Jay gives me one of those looks where you don't want to say it but you have to. "he is here to help. He is right, you can't control your power or your anger. You have become a danger and you need help."

I roll my eyes and get up. I start to get dressed into the clothes that Galina gave me. "What does he care? He probably has the power to take me out anyway." Jay says nothing.

"I'm your father, Daniel." I turn round to see him stood in the door way. "That's why I care."

At this point I'm not angry; I don't know how I feel. I take a gulp.

"There is someone I would like you to meet."

Jay raises an eyebrow. "Who?"

He motioned me to follow him. I look at Jay and he shrugs. I follow him out of the room and we walk past Valdameir. I come to a halt. "How is she?" He looks at me then to Dan Val Gule. "Valdameir, I'm sorry, okay? I didn't know."

He nods. "Daniel, I respect that, but before you had met her, I told you not to do this and you did it anyway."

Dan Val Gule steps closer to me and Jay pulls me closer to him. "He is just a boy, Valdameir, you can't expect him to follow all the rules." I mean, he isn't wrong.

"No, I can't, you are right, but if he cannot control himself, he cannot see her." He is right – I can't control myself.

"Valdameir, please forgive me." I will hate myself forever if he doesn't after all he has done for me.

"Daniel, I can forgive you for now, only because I know that you are just a boy who is struggling to get over his past."

I cry and punch the wall behind me then rest my head against it. "Why me?"

He walks up to me and places his hand on my shoulder. "Remember, it wasn't just you." He looks at Jay and I suddenly remember that I am being beyond selfish right now. "I will update you when I can, Daniel."

I nod at him and continue to follow Dan Val Gule. I walk out into the gardens and see the destruction I have caused. "Daniel, don't worry, you will know more soon."

We walk towards the end of the field and I suddenly come face to face with an incredibly large dragon. He has beautiful red shiny scales with black wings and stomach. I can't believe what

I am seeing. "His name is Vision." His head moved closer to me I started to panic a little but he nudges my tummy and I stroke his nose. This must be one of the best days of my life. He is the most beautiful creature I have ever seen.

Another one lands alongside him, yellow with a blue stripe going down the side and a white tummy. He also approaches me and nudges my arm. I also stroked his nose. "Jay are you seeing this?"

Jay walks closer and the yellow dragon turns his head to him. "I sure am and I still can't believe it." He smiles at me. "We have always wanted a dragon." He laughs. "It was actually our dream, remember?"

I smile at him. "Maybe dreams do come true after all." We both smile while petting the dragons. "Are they both yours?"

Dan Val Gule smiles at m.e "No, Valayrion here is Richard's, your uncle's dragon." Richard? That seems bit too normal.

"AKA, the Ripper." I look at Jay in slight shock.

"The Ripper? He's here?"

Dan Val Gule nods and points behind me. I turn to see the Ripper is standing right in front of me.

"He looks just like you, Val Gule."

Dan Val Gule laughs. "Handsome, then."

The Ripper walks closer to me. "Nah, he's a more handsome version of you; you're just fuck ugly." He smiles at Dan Val Gule.

"Wait, wait, I'm confused!" I look at Jay who is trying his best not to laugh. "So you are my father" –pointing at Dan Val Gule– "and you are my uncle?" The Ripper nods. "No, this can't be happening." I start to freak out a little bit.

"Daniel, hear him out." I look at Jay in shock. He comes over to me. "You have a chance to have a family, and more importantly I know he can help you control your anger. When your anger is under control even just a little, we can take back the fire nation." He holds up his pinky; I wrap my pinky round his.

"Promise me you won't leave me again."

He smiles. "Never."

I walk over to Dan Val Gule. "I'm willing to hear you out."

He nods and we head to the great hall to have a spot of lunch and a drink.

Jay

I look at Daniel's face as he sits there staring into space after hearing Dan Val Gule's story. "My mum tried to kill me?" Dan Val Gule nods. Tears come streaming down Daniel's face and he gets up from the table and starts pacing. "And it technically wasn't you that burnt down Whitefall, it was Vision?"

He nods again. "Vision was just as angry, as I was, only he was a literal dragon; there was no controlling him."

Daniel nods. He wants to deny all of it but he just stands there thinking. He looks at me. "And he told you all of this when he captured you?"

I look at Dan Val Gule, who looks confused. "Well, he didn't capture me. Richard slaughtered the camp I was in and pretty much saved me from the fate I was probably going to face. All I had to do was mention your name."

Richard has a massive smile on his face. "I do love slaughtering wanna-be armies." Dan Val Gule smiles at him.

"You said I'm too powerful for you to control, so you called in help?" Dan Val Gule nods. "Who?"

He sighs. "My older brother, Vang Chi."

I look at him, confused. "Who the fuck is that?"

Richard laughs. "Probably the best of my two brothers." Dan Val Gule gives Richard an evil glare. "What? It's true; we have had this argument."

He looks at him, furious. "And I have told you my side so we can further this conversation later."

Suddenly the doors fly open and a massive guy walks in, bigger than Dan Val Gule, very muscular, with dark brown hair and dark, almost black eyes with pale skin. I'm not going to lie, he is terrifying! I thought I was scared of Dan Val Gule! This guy is completely different. A slightly smaller guy comes in next to him, with light brown hair and blue eyes. "Hello, brother."

I look at Dan Val Gule. "That beast is your brother?"

Richard just sits there and smiles. I go to the same side as Richard and sit close to him for protection. Daniel doesn't move; he is completely frozen. "Vang Chi."

I lean in to Richard. "You never said your brother was a monster."

Vang Chi looks directly at me. "Who's this idiot?"

I take a massive gulp. "I am Jay, co-general of the British fire nation army."

He smiles. "What army? I don't see one. What about you, Vince?" The guy next to him shakes his head.

"Well, it's complicated."

Daniel stands there just looking at him. He looks at Dan Val Gule. "This is my uncle?" Richard nods at him. Daniel smiles. "I think I win, Jay."

I roll my eyes. "Fuck you, Daniel."

He laughs. "I don't think you're gonna find a bloke scarier than that, do you?" I shake my head. "And I don't think I have ever seen you run so fast." His smile is even bigger. "And that is my fucking uncle!"

Richard laughs as Dan Val Gule stands there looking at him angry. "Yes, well, he's not staying for long."

Vang Chi laughs. "This is your boy? The one you need help with?"

Daniel looked slightly offended "Help with? Really?"

I can feel Daniel getting angry. "So, I'm going to take cover."

Vang Chi looks at him. "You have a little bit of cheek," he squares up to Daniel, "talking to your uncle like that."

Daniel smiles and his fists light up.

"Vang Chi, stop, he can't control it." He looks down at Daniel's fists then his whole arm starts lighting up. Vang Chi takes a step back in shock as his eyes light up on fire.

"Where is she?" He looks at me. It's like he's a different person.

"Um, she is in her room resting at the moment but I'm sure she will be able to see you soon."

His whole body is on fire now. "Jay, I want to see her now."

I gulp. "You know Valdameir will never let you in like this – you have to calm down in order to see her. I know you have found out a lot today and your head is over-loading but you need to calm down."

He closes his eyes and takes a deep breath. The fire starts to go out and his eyes go back to normal. He falls into Vang Chi's arms. Dan Val Gule and Richard run over. He is awake but very tired.

"What was that?"

Vang Chi hands him to Dan Val Gule and looks over to me. "I need to see this woman, now."

I take him to Gemma's room and knock on the door.

"Who is it?" She sounds very poorly.

"It's Jay. I have a guest that needs to see you."

Valdameir opens the door. "Who's this?" I looked at him, terrified. "Jay, what's happened?"

I fall into his arms. "Valdameir, this guy needs to talk to Gemma, just trust me." He nods and lets us in.

Vang-Chi

"All right, Vince, come at me." He comes charging towards me, throws in a punch. I swiftly move my head to the side, bend down, grip him by the legs and pin him to the floor.

"You're a cunt, Vang-Chi."

I get up and hold my hand out to pull him up. We get into position again to continue training when a massive gust of wind comes over. I look up and see a dragon slowly landing. It is Valayrion. He lands and nudges my shoulder. I give him a stroke and a little peck, which I know he hates but I do it anyway. He moved his head and I see Richard stood next to him.

"Hello, little brother." He rolls his eyes. I walk up to him and wrap him in my arms. I pull away and put my hand on his shoulder. "How are you?"

He smiles at me. "Struggling, but I'm getting there."

I motion him to follow me. "Vince, get the chef to make us some lunch."

Vince nods and goes to give the order. We go into my tent, which is huge – most of it was stolen, to be fair. It has three parts to; it the bathroom, the bedroom, which has a very comfortable king size bed in it, and the lounge area which has two sofas, a fire place, table and two chairs.

"Wow, Vang-Chi, you have done well."

I laugh. "Nah, most of it is stolen." He looks at me, shocked.

The chef comes in with two plates, both with ham, egg and chips. "Thank you, mate." He smiles and bows. I walk over to the table, pour me and Richard a drink each, then sit down. Richard sits next to me and starts digging in. "So, to what do I owe this pleasure?"

He wipes his mouth. "I need your help."

I pick up a chip and stuff it in my mouth while looking at him. "What have you done?"

He laughs. "Well, it's not quite what I've done, it's what Dan Val Gule has done."

I roll my eyes. "Not interested. He can suffer."

He takes a sip of his drink. "He's had a son."

I stop in my tracks and stare at him for a minute. "With who? He's an ugly cunt."

Richard laughs. "With some whore named Mary."

I roll my eyes. "How convenient she has the same name as nan."

Richard laughs a little. "His name is Daniel; he is the Great British general of the fire nation and extremely strong."

I knew that was coming. "And his own father can't help him why?" I pour myself another drink.

"Because he is beyond Val Gule's power and knowledge. We fear he might have done something to the water nation general."

I raise my eyebrow. "What, like beat him up or something because that is normal."

Richard laughs and downs his drink. "It is a her, and no. Basically, she is a very poorly girl at the moment. She has been having sex with him."

I spit out my drink. "That's not possible! She should be dead."

Richard nods. "Naturally, yeah, she should, but she is very poorly."

I sit there frozen. "I will be there in a few hours."

Richard smiles at me. "I hope you will stay, Vang Chi. I'm planning on staying. I miss my big brother."

I smile. I have always gotten along with Richard and I do know that he struggles a lot, especially as I have left him with Val Gule. I walk Richard out to Valayrion and watch him fly off.

"Vince, pack up the army, we go to the water nation house."

He looks at me, confused, but he does so anyway.

We arrive outside the house and already I could can something has happened here, not to mention there is a gigantic ice wall splitting the fire nation and the water nation apart. I get off my horse and push open the doors. Vince and I walk in. I see Dan Val Gule and Richard sitting at the table with a young lad who looks at me, terrified. I look back to Val Gule and grin.

"Hello, brother."

Richard can't wipe that smirk off his face.

"That beast is your brother!"

I look at the small lad who makes a beeline for Richard.

"Vang Chi." I continue to smile.

"You never said your brother was a monster."

I sort of feel a little insulted. "Who's this idiot?"

He sits up so quick it is actually quite amusing. "I'm Jay, co-general of the Great British fire nation army." That's funny, I will admit.

"What army? I don't see one. What about you, Vince?" Vince shakes his head.

"Well, it's complicated." I can't wait to hear all about it.

"This is my uncle?" I look at the guy standing up. Ge is a very good looking lad, but definitely Val Gule's boy; he looks exactly like him. He smiles. "I think I win, Jay." I raise my eyebrows.

"Fuck you, Daniel."

Daniel laughs. "I don't think your gonna find a bloke scarier than that, do you?" I have a gigantic grin on my face. "That is my fucking uncle." Richard laughs, Val Gule just looks angry.

"Yes, well he's not staying for long." Richard looks at him, saddened. I just laugh.

"This is your boy? The one you need help with?" I can feel quite a lot of power, but it isn't coming from me.

"Help with? Really?" I grow a little concerned.

"So, I'm going to take cover."

I can't stop looking at Daniel. "You have a little bit of cheek," I decide to see how far he has already gone so I square up to him, "talking to your uncle like that." He smiles at me and his fists light up on fire.

"Vang Chi, stop, he can't control it."

I look down and can see the fire starts traveling up his arms. I look up to see his eyes are literal flames. I step back in shock.

"Where is she?"

I looked at Richard, who is white.

"Um, she is in her room resting at the moment but I'm sure she will be able to see you soon." Jay is trying his best, bless him, but his whole body is now up in flames.

"Jay, I want to see her now."

Oh dear god, I have never seen anything like it.

"You know Valdameir will never let you in like this – you have to calm down in order to see her. I know you have found out a lot today and your head is over-loading but you need to calm down."

He closes his eyes, takes a deep breath the fire starts to go out. He must really love this girl. He falls forwards. I catch him just before he hits the floor. Val Gule and Richard come running over. "What was that?"

I hand him over to Val Gule then look to Vince; he is white. I look round to Jay. "I need to see this woman, now."

Jay nods and motions me to follow him. We arrive outside some double doors with five water nation soldiers and two fire nation soldiers standing outside. Jay knocks on the door. "Who is it?"

Jay sighs as I look at him. "It's Jay. I have a guest that needs to see you."

This man opens the door. "Who is this?" He's going to be a dead man if he thinks he is going to stop me getting in. "Jay, what's happened?"

Jay falls into this man's arms; you can tell he is terrified. "Valdameir, this guy needs to talk to Gemma, just trust me."

He nods. I walk in and what I see makes my heart drop. She looks so fragile, so poorly. I need to help her. I definitely need to stay. Daniel is beyond Val Gule's help; I'm his only hope.

Gemma

A rather large man walks in and looks at me, saddened. "Oh, bless you." He walks closer to me. "He wants to see you."

I smile at him. "And I want to see him." I start to cry. "Please get him."

He looks at Valdameir. "He has to see her; I won't be able to help control him if you won't let him see her."

Valdameir looks at me and nods, Jay runs out to get Daniel.

"What's your name?" I ask him. He looks at me and smiles. He has quite a warm smile.

"Vang Chi, my lady," he says as he takes my hand and gives it a peck. "Don't worry, you will be better in no time."

Daniel runs through the door and looks at me.

"Daniel."

He walks over to me slowly. "Did I do this?" He places his hand on my cheek and sits next to me. I place my hand on his leg.

"No you didn't. Don't worry, I'm fine. I already feel that little bit better now you're here."

Vang Chi walks up to him. "He needs some time alone with her, then we will start tomorrow with the training, okay?" Daniel nods at him and they all leave the room.

"This is my fault."

I sit myself up and place my hand on his cheek. "No, its not. What I saw was scary, yes," he looks at me and places his forehead on mine, "but awesome."

I smile. He kisses me on the lips and then moves his hand

down to my breast. He moves away. "I don't want to hurt you again." He moves his hand down to my hip. "More importantly, I don't want to kill you; I can't live without you."

I grab his hand and pull him closer to me. "You won't." I kiss him on the lips. "You have already made me stronger."

He smiles at me. "I just can't help it, you're like my drug. When I can't see you or have you close, I lose control."

I smile at him and open the covers, motioning for him to join me. He strips off but doesn't re move his underwear and gets into bed next to me. I rest my head on his chest and he cradles me in his arms. "You know what that's called?"

He turns over to face me. "What?"

I smile at him and touch his cheek. "Love."

He pulls me close and kisses me. I look up at him. "I love you, Gemma." I smile. He holds me in his arms as we lie there in silence. "Gemma, you know you mentioned that my eyes went red while I was having sex with you?" I nod, wondering where he is going with this. "Last time we had sex your eyes went an icy blue." What the fuck? Icy blue? That's a bit on the weird side.

"Icy Blue?"

He nods. "I guess that means neither of us are normal."

I sigh and hold him even tighter. "I wish I was. I wish we were normal sometimes."

He smiles at me and places his hand on my ass to pull me in closer. I can feel his erection touching my vagina. "You're a little bit on the horny side."

He laughs. "I'm currently in bed with the woman I love."

I kiss him. "Show me how much you love me."

He smiles then slides his hand down my body and inserts his fingers into my vagina. "Ah!" I wrap my arms around his neck and he slides down to kiss my breasts. I hold on to his head as I moan in pleasure. He kisses further down my body until he reaches my vagina he sticks his tongue straight in with no warning. "Oh Daniel." I grip his hair so tight. "Oh keep going!" He grabs my wrists and pins them down to the sides but he doesn't stop there. He stops and walks off to find something. I am bit confused. "Why did you stop?"

He smiles. "You asked me to show you, so I am going to give you the best sex you have ever had."

He gets four dressing gown ties and ties me down to the bed then he finds a blind fold and places it on my head. He looks me in the eyes and this time I notice his eyes aren't red. "You ready?" I nod and he place the blind fold over my eyes.

Daniel

After I place the blind fold over her eyes, I look at her, slightly scared. I pray to the dragon sprit that he will let it be me that shows her love and not my power. I climb on top of her and kiss her on the neck. "I love you," I whisper in her ear. I tuck her hair behind her ear and kiss her on the lips. I kiss down her body and take my place back between her legs. I go back to licking her. She tastes amazing. I run my hands all over her body, especially her breasts. Her body feels amazing; her skin is so smooth. She continues to moan as I stop at her stomach. I feel attached to that area of her body and I don't know why. I kiss it and move my way up slowly, still feeling attached to that area of her body

While fingering her I don't feel any surge of power or anything; I feel in control. I kiss her breast so lightly. "Ready?"

She nods. I thrust my penis in. "AH!"

I start to move slowly. I place one hand on her hip and another on her cheek. "Mm yes!" Then I go in harder and faster until I am pounding her so hard I could break her.

"Oh yes Daniel!" I move my hand to the top of her vagina and start to rub. Her moans are so load I'm sure the whole house can hear her.

"Say my name," I whisper in her ear.

"Yes Daniel!"

I'm not satisfied. "Louder."

She is receiving so much pleasure she can't talk. "OH DANIEL!" That's what I'm talking about. She is griping onto the dressing gown ties so hard you can see her muscles.

"Oh don't stop!"

I release inside her and slow down. I untie her arms and take off her blind fold. "That was just me, no power, nothing."

She smiles. "And it was just as good as the previous times."

I smile at her and untie her legs. She moves up the bed. I grab the duvet and tuck her in.

"Will you stay with me tonight please?" I smile at her and slip myself into the other side of the bed. She moves closer to me. "I love you too, Daniel."

I wrap her in my arms and smile. I start to dose off when there is a knock at the door. "It's Jay."

Gemma sits up a little. "Come in."

He walks through the door then grins but his grin slowly fades. "Phillip is here."

I look at Gemma, tuck her hair behind her ear and kiss her on the forehead. "Stay here." I get up and get dressed into my general's uniform. I mean business now. She smiles at me. "Promise me you will stay?"

She nods. I kiss her on the forehead then auto-drive touch her stomach. I walk out the room with Jay and shut the door. "Guard this door with your life." They nod.

I walk into the great hall and Phillip is standing there with a few soldiers from my army and a few I don't recognize. "You were too stubborn to die, then." My father, both of my uncles and Valdameir appear from the other side of the hall. "What do you want, Phillip?"

He grins. "Nice, you have Dan Val Gule, the ripper and whoever this is on your side as well as Valdameir."

I roll my eyes. "I asked you a question. Being your general, you are required to answer me."

He laughs. "Oh please, Daniel, I could destroy you with just a name."

I laugh at him. "Really, and who's that?"

He grins. "Charles Knight."

My whole body freezes and my father, both my uncles and Valdameir look at me. I look up at Phillip and grin. "That name will no longer haunt me, because I, Daniel, am the Great British general of the fire nation." I walk closer to Phillip. "I will get my army back and I will find your leader and your leader will wish he had never been born." Jay walks a fair distance away from me but goes round the group slightly.

"With what army?"

I look round at my father and both my uncles. They all grin and walk up behind me. "Introducing my family. I have three armies and two dragons all willing to fight for me." He gulps. I smile. "You didn't see that one coming, did ya? My father is the one and only Dan Val Gule." I can feel my father grinning at me in the background. "My uncles are the Ripper and Vang Chi – no one has heard of him because he is that good at going undercover" My smile is even bigger. "So tell me, Phillip? What am I facing?" He gulps and looks at Valdameir. "Oh yeah, that's a bonus! I have Valdameir on my side." Valdameir stands there so proud. "Not to mention her ladyship."

Phillip rolls his eyes. "She's beautiful, I will admit, my lord, but how long will it take you to kill her? You think someone like you can be general, someone with so much damage from his past?" Okay, he has stepped over the line.

"I have a lot more right than you Phillip."

He laughs at me. "I will not rest, Daniel, until everything is how it should be."

I look at my dad. "How's that?" Do I want to know the

answer to this question?

"Well, these guys dead" –pointing at my dad, Valdameir and my uncles– "you and Jay safely returned to Charles and her ladyship where she should be – in the kitchens."

Vang Chi, my dad and Richard crack up laughing. "OH MY GOD THAT IS JUST HILARIOUS!" Vang Chi says while holding onto his stomach. Phillip looks at them, angry. "You actually think you can take us three on?"

My dad walks up beside me and puts his arm around my shoulder. "What's even funnier is you think I'm going to allow my son to be in the hands of this Charles."

Phillip laughs. "He hasn't told you, has he?" I look at him, confused and angry. "He was Charles's lover."

My dad grips my shoulder and continues to look at Phillip but now he is angry. He must know some of the story. "You're pushing your luck, boy. You best leave before I remove your head from your shoulders." I look at my dad. I have to admit I am shaking a little bit, not because of anger but because I am scared at this point. I am glad I have him.

Jay walks up next to Richard to revise some reassurance that he is safe. William walks in and stands next to me. "Ah, William, you're a traitor as well then I see?" I look to William.

"No, I am loyal. I have remained by my general's side, as these boys should have done."

Phillip grins. "Your poor wife is missing you dearly." William's eyes widen. "Did you know she is pregnant?"

Tears start leaving William's eyes. He looks to me for support. I look at the members of my army. "You boys have a choice: fight alongside this wanna-be leader and die or come back to me and live, it's up to you."

They whisper to each other and Derek approaches me. "We

choose Phillip." Then he winks at me and smiles and makes a piece sign, meaning either two hours or two days.

"Very well, looks like it's death then." He walks back over to the men.

"See, I'm already better than you." The idiot fell for it.

"See you boys on the battle field." I start to walk off.

"I hear her ladyship is unwell." I stop on the spot. "Give her my love, won't you."

I walk off to Gemma's room to find her up and out of bed. "Feeling better then?"

She smiles. "I am indeed." She walks up to me and smiles, wraps her arms around me and gives me a kiss.

"You okay?" I looked at her weird.

"Yeah, of course, just happy I'm out of bed and ready to actually do my job again." She kisses me then walks out the room. That was weird.

Gemma

Daniel walks out the room. I can't help but notice when he was kissing my body, he only really kissed around one area and that is the area he held that night. He also touched my stomach as he left.

"Well that was just beautiful."

I jump out of my skin to see a man sat in the corner of my room. He comes out from the shadows and I can see he is huge, with dirty blonde hair, pale skin and blue eyes.

"Relax, my lady, I'm not going to harm you." Not even remotely comforting. He sits on the edge on my bed and touches my stomach. "You, my lady, have become a problem."

I gulp. "How?"

He pours himself a drink and smiles. "Do you know how dangerous it is having sex with a fire manipulator, let alone someone as powerful as Daniel?" I look at him and shake my head. "You, my lady, are lucky to be alive, but I think I might know why. But that is a story for another day." I look at him, confused. "If you survive the birth, you really are who I think you are, then we will have a bigger problem."

My eyes widen. "Wait, what birth?"

He smiles at me. "Oh yes, you're pregnant, my dear." He puts down his drink and crawls on top of me, causing the covers to drop and revel my breasts. He looks down and smiles. He cups one and kisses it. He cups the other one and starts to massage them. He moves his hand up and down my body, touching everything. I am frozen at this point. He comes up to my ear and holds my neck. I cry, petrified of what he could do to me next.

"You are just as beautiful as the last time I saw you." He hugs me, removes the duvet, takes one last look at my body then kisses me on the cheek then moves round and kisses me on the lips. "I have to go. Until we meet again."

Who is that and what does he mean the last time he saw me? I sit on the edge of my bed frozen. I held the breast he touched in my hand and decided to make my way to the shower to wash off his stench. I scrub that breast so hard that it goes red then I hold my stomach. Now it all makes sense – Daniel wasn't just protecting me he was protecting our baby too.

I walk to my wardrobe and find a dress to wear. I think if he is telling the truth I have to wear something lose around the middle. I think about holding our baby in my arms, about how protective Daniel is. I think about our life together and how it would work. It all makes me smile and forget about what just happened.

Daniel walked in the room to see me up and dressed. "Feeling better then?"

I smile at him. I do love his fire nation uniform. "I am indeed." I walk up close to him and wrap my arms around him and give him a kiss.

He places his hands on my hips. "You okay?" He gives me a funny look.

"Yeah, of course, just happy I'm out of bed and ready to actually do my job again." I kiss him then walk out the room. I go straight to see the doctor.

"Ah, my lady, you're looking much better."

I smile at him. "Thank you!" I sit down opposite him. "I was wondering if you could do something for me." He looks at me, intrigued. "Could you do an ultrasound or something on my stomach? Daniel is attracted to something and I need to know what it is."

He leads me over to the table and I reveal my stomach. He puts on some cold gel and places this weird looking object on my stomach. "I think I know why he is attracted to it, my lady." I look at him. "You're pregnant."

I look at the doctor, shocked. He turned the screen to show me. "See them two bits there, shaped like a kidney bean?" I nod. "You're having twins, my lady."

My eyes widen. "Twins?" He nods. "How far along am I?"

He looks at the screen. "I would say two months, so you will have about six or seven months left of your pregnancy." He looks bit on the worried side.

"What is it?"

He looks at me. "I will pop in every week, my lady, and monitor the babies. only because they are twins and I am assuming Daniel is the father." I nod. "My lady, you are in a bit of a sticky situation. The likelihood of you dying at birth is very high." I look at him in shock. I am in a bit of a sticky situation.

Derek

"Get up, we have an army to assemble." I smack John round the head with a pillow.

He slowly opens his eyes and rolls over. "How do you plan on doing that, with a wave of a magic wand?"

I sigh then collapse on the bed next to him. "John, how do we expect our wives and children to be safe when we have a leader like Phillip?" He turns round and faces me.

"Derek, it's impossible; loads of men have tried to venture to the water nation but Phillip has found out and either killed them or imprisoned them." He has a point.

"Listen, we need to think about how we will die. I would much rather die loyal to Daniel than be roasted alive by a flying dragon made out of fire." He looks at me. "Daniel needs his army, John; we have to take back the fire nation and too many men are ill or dying."

He smiles. "I've got to admit, the dragon that Daniel produced was very cool."

I laugh. "Let's go." We sneak out of the tents that the original army have been placed in and persuade a few more soldiers and their wives to come with us. We make sure we get William's wife Elenor as well. Since Phillip has taken over, the fire nation has fallen apart; new men were brought in and Daniel's army was cast out of their homes into tents and given new uniforms to wear. We all place on our previous uniform that we wore when Daniel was general and make our way down to the dungeons. They are always guarded by Phillip's men – that's how much he doesn't trust us, and rightly so. The prisons are based underneath the general's house; you have to be a fire manipulator to enter the hall with all the cells inside. We manage to sneak past all the men to the door leading to the prison.

"What's the plan? And please remember we have a fair few pregnant women with us, including my wife."

I gesture him to follow along with the other men. I place my hand onto the statue of the dragon and the doors slide open. We make our way downstairs and see three of Phillip's men talking. We stop and listen in to the conversation. "So did Siri tell you, the general survived." They don't look surprised.

"Doesn't surprise me at all; they say he's stronger than he looks." They all laugh. "If Phillip fails him again, he's going to die. He knows that." Fails who? "All he wants is Jay back and the general dead, it's not that hard." Jay back and the general dead? I have so many questions but our main focus right now is getting Daniel back, his army and our women safe.

I look at John, concerned. "Come on." We make our way down the stairs and confront the soldiers.

"Evening, boys. Phillip would like us to take over."

He laughs. "Phillip is stupid, but not that stupid. He wouldn't put a bunch of soldiers like you down here."

I shrug. "Very well." I quickly snap his neck and the other two come charging at me. John and Henry, another soldier, jump straight in front of me. John slices open one of their throats and Henry smashes the other one into the wall so hard it cracks his skull leaving blood pouring out of his nose and mouth. We grab the keys and open the doors to all the cells. You can tell some of the men have been in here a fair while and some only recently.

"Derek, you could get killed for this!"

I pick up one of the men and look at Liam. "I am willing to risk it if it means my wife and children will be safe."

I turn round. A shadow of a man is walking towards us. He walks round the corner and it is merely an old man, with messy grey hair, trousers that looked far too small for him and a striped shirt. His glasses sit on the end of his nose. "You boys look like you could use some help." I nod. "Follow me."

I start to follow when John stops me. "How do we know we can trust him?" The man stops and turns around.

"We have to try." Jojn nods and we walk over to him. He smiles and leads us down to these caves. "I had no idea these were here."

He laughs. "Daniel and Jay used to hide in them all the time." I look at him, confused. "They practised their fire manipulating here."

We reach the river dividing the water nation and the fire nation, which is one huge river. I look to the right and see a load of Phillip's men guarding the fire nation side of the river. I look to the left and see the water nation watch tower looking over the river. He turns to me. "Wait for it." I step forwards slightly and before I know it a load of men come charging over from the water nation. They aren't water manipulators or fire manipulators, they are wearing red battle uniforms with a dragon symbol on the top of the sleeve. The old man turns to me. "Listen to me, I need you to deliver a message to Daniel." I nod. "Tell him that I wish to see him in three days' time in the middle of the forest, alone." I gulp and nod. He gestures us to move then heads to join the fight.

"Who the fuck was that?" I look at John then back at the army in the distance fighting Phillip's army.

"I don't know but I have a funny feeling." I make sure all the men get past then follow on.

Gemma

I sit at the dinner table next to Daniel and look down at my plate. Tonight, is fish pie with mash and peas. I start to feel bit on the nauseous side. I start to push the peas around my plate trying to assess whether I am going to be sick of not.

"You okay?"

I look at Daniel, give him a small smile and nod. I then start to feel it coming with no warning. I get up and make a runner for the nearest bathroom and hang my head over the toilet. Galina comes in after me, followed by Daniel and Valdameir. She rubs my back and holds my hair as I vomit in the bathroom.

"Boys, go and wait outside please." They nod and go and wait outside and leave me and Galina in the toilets. "That's it, darling, let it all out." I manage to get it all out then fall into Galina's arms. "Is there something I need to know, darling?"

I start to cry then gain the strength to look at her. "I'm pregnant, Galina."

She looks at me in shock and pulls me back in for a hug. "It's okay, daring, it's okay."

I cry hysterically in her arms. "Can you get Valdameir please? I need him."

She nods. She knows that whenever I am upset, I always turn to Valdameir and always want to be in his arms.

"What's is wrong, my dear?" He crouches down next to me and I lean into him. He wraps his arms around me. "Talk to me?"

I can't stop crying. This morning I was so happy but now I

can't stop thinking about what the doctor said. "Please don't be mad, I just don't know what to do." Galina comes around the other side and tucks my hair behind my ear.

"Shhh, it's okay. I will try not to be but I can't promise anything." I hold him tight and bury my head in his chest.

"I'm pregnant."

I can feel him heat up slightly. "WHAT?"

I start to panic. "Valdameir, I'm sorry, I didn't think it was possible for a water manipulator to have a fire manipulator's child." He looks at me and sees how scared I am.

His anger drops and he hugs me even tighter. "What do you want to do?"

I look at him. "I don't know." I grip his uniform and continue to cry. "I'm not normal, am I?"

Tears start streaming down Galina's face. "Come on, let's get you to bed." He gets up then takes my hand.

"I just want to be normal."

He smiles. "Normal is no fun." I laugh and he walks me out the door and Daniel is waiting outside.

"Are you okay?"

Valdameir gives him an angry look. "She is just bit poorly. She will be okay." He pulls me away from Daniel and starts walking me to my room.

"VALDAMEIR STOP!" I turn round and I can see Daniel is angry. Galina pulls me away from Valdameir and two of my soldiers' step in front of us to protect us.

"Yes, Daniel?" I have to admit he is good at keeping his cool.

"My girlfriend has just chucked her guts up in there and you're not going to tell me what's going on? Don't you think I have a right to know?"

Dan Val Gule looks at Daniel in shock then steps forwards.

"Enough secrecy, Valdameir, what's going on?"

He rolls his eyes then looks at me. I hide in Galina's arms. "If you really must know, your SON here has gotten her pregnant." Daniel's eyes widen and he looks at me in shock.

I fall to the floor and cry. Daniel walks up to me but Valdameir stops him. "Not yet, Daniel. Come and see her tomorrow morning, okay?"

Daniel looks at him with rage then Jay comes up behind him. "He just found out she's pregnant and you're stopping him from seeing her? She's not a little girl anymore, Valdameir."

Daniel looks like he's about to kill him. I look up at Daniel. "I'm sorry I didn't tell you. I was scared and didn't know what to do." I start to hyperventilate.

Galina steps in front of them. "We all need to calm down; it is not good for her and not good for the baby."

I look down at the floor. "Babies."

Valdameir darts his attention back to me. "WHAT? BABIES!"

I nod at him. "Can you just take me to bed please!"

He looks at Daniel then at Galina. "Darling this is not good for her. You are only making it worse. Let's just take her to bed then return to the situation in the morning." Valdameir nods.

"Daniel, I'm just going to take her to bed and calm her down, okay? She will talk when she is asleep."

He nods and leans down to kiss me on the forehead. "Goodnight, baby. I will see you in the morning." I nod. "I love you."

I give him a relieved look. "Really? Still?" He smiles and laughs a little. "I love you too."

Valdameir picks me up and takes me to my room. I sit on the edge of my bed and he looks at me. "I will talk to you about this in the morning but I am not happy, you know that, right?"

I nod at him. "You're disappointed." He looks at me and smiles. "I know I'm not normal, Valdameir. Who am I?"

He sits next to me as Galina stares at him. "You will learn in your own time. Right now, you are not ready." I nod at him. "Get some sleep; you need it." He kisses me on the forehead and walks out the room. Galina smiles and gives me a massive hug and follows. I get into my nice big oversized blue jumper and get into bed.

Dan Val Gule

I cannot believe what I have just heard. She is pregnant with twins. "Look at that, Val Gule, you have found your son and now you're going to be a grandad. Aren't you lucky!"

I shoot a look at Vang Chi, who has a massive grin on his face. "You really think this is a laughing matter?"

He shrugs. Daniel is pacing the hall; you can tell he is freaking out a little. "Daniel, relax! It will be fine!"

He gives a pissed-off laugh. "Jay, when have you ever known Valdameir to say we need to talk and it be a good talk?" Jay knows that Daniel is in trouble. "I won't even know the first thing about being a dad."

I roll my eyes. "We are all here to help you, Daniel, don't worry."

Valdameir walks into the hall with Galina. "Do you realise what you have done?"

Daniel looks at him, terrified. "Is she okay?"

Valdameir laughs. "OF COURSE, SHE'S NOT! SHE IS TERRIFIED!" All I can think about is how she got pregnant in the first place. "YOU, DANIEL, HAVE SENTENCED THAT GIRL TO DEATH!" Tears start streaming down his face.

"What do you mean? He just had sex with her and got her pregnant, so what?" Jay is brave; he looks at Valdameir then makes a beeline for Vang Chi.

"Water manipulators can't bear fire manipulators' children; if they do, they will die either during pregnancy or at birth."

Daniel looks horrified.

"They can't be Daniel's."

He looks at me, confused and worried. "What do you mean?" Daniel is scared and it worries me.

"You have to be a fire manipulator to bear Daniel's children. Because of his blood line it is impossible for Daniel to get a water manipulator pregnant."

Valdameir looks at me so angry you can feel the heat from here. "So, you're calling her a liar?"

I nod. "I think she cheated. She just wants Daniel as the father because he's powerful and she needs his help to lead an army."

Valdameir smiles. "You, Dan Val Gule, have no idea who she is."

Daniel steps in front of me. "You heard what he said; it's impossible, so how do I know they're mine?" Vang Chi gives me a pissed-off look, he's not happy with me at all.

"I BEG YOUR PARDON, YOUNG MAN!" Galina approaches him and is fuming. "HOW DARE YOU EVEN THINK SHE IS CAPABLE OF DOING THAT!" She gets right up to Daniel's face that.

I step forwards. "She's a woman; she has no idea what's she's doing and has no right to lead an army, so she decides to cheat on Daniel and claim that they are his so that he will help her lead. I'm not having any of it!"

Valdameir comes so close to me I can feel his breath. "I know they are Daniel's babies but Dan Val Glue, I will warn you, you are messing with forces you don't want to mess with."

I give him an evil glare. "Daniel will never see her again."

Daniel and Jay look at me in shock. "Dad, you cannot just come into my life and tell me what to do. I am twenty-three tomorrow; I can make the decision for myself, thank you." He looks at Valdameir. "May I speak with her tomorrow at least."

He nods then glares back at me. I decide to pay Gemma a little visit. I knock on the door, expecting her to still be asleep.

"Who is it?" She clearly can't sleep.

"Dan Val Gule, my lady."

All four of her soldiers look at me. "Come in." I open the door and one of them stops me.

"Keep the door open, my lord." I tug my arm back but respect their wishes.

"You have some very over-protective soldiers, my lady."

She lies there in a blue jumper still crying. She can't even look at me. "They are only doing their jobs." I sit on the edge of the bed, watch the tears fall from her eyes onto her bed sheets. "You probably think I'm a scumbag, a liar, and I don't blame you."

I wouldn't say that, exactly. "Here, I brought you some elderflower tea."

She sits up in her bed, her eyes all puffy and red. "I'm scared, okay. I didn't think this could happen. He's a fire manipulator and I'm a water manipulator." She takes a sip of her tea and starts to cry again.

"Truth is, Gemma, it is impossible for a water manipulator to bear Daniel's children because of his blood line."

She puts her cup down on the table and looks at me. "Then why me? I just want a normal life, Dan Val Gule. Why can my life never be normal?" She is hurting; she doesn't even know herself. "I just want to be back in Russia, walking along the river." She laughs and smiles at the thought. "Valdameir having a go at me all the time." She looks at me again. "Galina doing my hair all the time even though I hated it." I smile. "But no, I am the general of the Great British water nation, letting my army down all the time because I am too unwell to do anything." I shake my head "I sleep with a very powerful fire nation general and end up pregnant with his babies and now I might die." She curls up and hugs her knees. "The sad thing is I don't know what to do anymore. I love Daniel so much."

I sigh and look at her because I know deep down, she is not lying and she is just scared. "Listen, you are not letting your men down; I can tell each and every one of them love you and will fight for you until the death." I take her hand. "I can tell that you do love Daniel. What worries me is how this happened because it is never meant to happen, which obviously makes me question it." She gives me an evil glare.

"I never cheated on him. You can ask every man in this house – no man ever entered my room. I spent ninety percent of my time with Daniel. When he was out, all I could think about was him and before him, I had never slept with another man." I know she is telling the truth, I am just in denial. "I know you're scared, but how do you think I feel? I'm fucking terrified." She has a point. "I'm literally going to die." Again, another point. I do feel sorry for her.

"Do you want me to get Daniel?"

She nods and I walk out the room to get Daniel.

William

I literally can't stop thinking about what Phillip said. I decide to take a walk and sit on the stone steps leading down to the once beautiful garden until Daniel destroyed it, but the gardeners have been working on making it beautiful again.

"You ok?" I turn to see Dean, the captain of the water nation. I give him a small smile. He sits down next to me. "Rough day?"

I laugh. "More like a rough few months."

He laughs. "Listen, I'm on my way home, why don't you come to mine for dinner? I'm sure my wife will be fine with it."

I smile and nod. We make our way down to this small cottage. Outside are bright green bushes covered in roses and a small wooden gate. As we walk through and Dean opens the door, we walk into this huge living room. There is a plasma TV in the corner next to the window, which looks out to the general's house. Next to it is a stone fire place which already has a fire lit. It is lovely and warm. The sofas are a rich brown colour made out of fabric. They have a white fluffy rug; on top of it lies a beautiful black pug. It registers that Dean is home and comes running up to him.

"Hey, boy!" It is male – okay, got it! He is so excited; maybe I should get Elenor a dog when I see her again.

"Honey, I'm home!" This beautiful woman comes strolling into the living room. She has her pyjamas on. She has long blonde hair and blue eyes. She is quite chunky and has olive skin.

"Honey, I didn't realise we were having guests, otherwise I

would have changed."

I smile at her as she approaches. "Honestly, its fine, my wife does it all the time." She smiles then notices I am in my fire nation uniform.

"I'm his captain."

She looks to Dean. "Well, welcome to our humble home! Would you like a tea or coffee?" I honestly thought she was going to kick me out.

"Honey, I will make it. Please sit down." I smile at him.

"Darling, I may be pregnant but while I can still move around, I'm making the most of it." Dean rolls his eyes then I remember what Phillip said about Elenor. I really hope it's not true because that is not how I wanted to find out.

I walk into the kitchen; it is lovely, only small with black marble sides, a breakfast bar, a large wooden table and chairs. It is beautiful. "You have a lovely home, Elenor. Would love a place like this."

She smiles. "My name is Sandy, by the way." She holds out her hand and I shake it. I sit at the table with Dean who is reading the news.

"The world is still falling apart then?"

Sandy laughs. "You are Gemma's captain and you have only just worked that one out?" Dean laughs.

"Thank you for having me, I really appreciate it."

Dean smiles at me and raises his eyebrows. "Well, I thought I would pull you way from all the drama."

I laugh and shrug. "Yeah, well it does just get worse and worse."

He laughs at me Sandy presents a full roast dinner. I do love a good roast. We sit there eating our meal when the door goes.

"I'll get it." Dean gets up and walks to the door. I finish up my meal as Dean walks back in with two water nation soldiers. He looks at me. "You will never believe it." I stand up, looking at him with so much hope. "Daniel's army have escaped. Some are injured and they have also all brought their wives with them."

My eyes widen. I look at Sandy. She just smiles at me. "Thank you so much for the roast, I thoroughly enjoyed it."

She stops me. "Go and get her. Also, bring her back; I want to meet her."

I look to Dean. "Thank you." He smiles.

"GO!" I jump as Sandy shouts at me. I bolt out the door and up to the gardens to see the army somewhere being treated. Some look like they haven't eaten a decent meal in weeks. I look to see John and Derek who are talking to Jay.

"John!" I run up to John and give him a massive hug. I would do the same with his wife but I don't like her. He pulls away and smiles.

"WILLIAM!" I know that voice. I turn to see Elenor. I run up to her, pick her up and twirl her around. We hold each other so tight.

I give her a massive kiss then move my hand down to her stomach. "Is it true?"

She has tears in her eyes as she nods her head. "Is that okay?"

I laugh and cry at the same time; I am so happy. "YES, YES! OF COURSE, IT IS!" I wrap her back in my arms.

"William," oh dear god, "I shouldn't have but I wanted to surprise you; I know the gender of the baby." Oh good, at least it's only one baby. I smile at her. "It's a boy."

I kiss her so hard and place my hand on her stomach again. "I love you, Elenor. I have missed you so much."

She places her forehead on mine. "I love you too, William. I am so proud of you."

I smile. Dean walks up next to me and I notice he has Sandy with him. "Elenor, this is Dean and his wife Sandy. Dean is the captain of the water nation."

He takes Elenor's hand and gives it a peck. "It's an honour to meet you. William has told me a lot about you."

She smiles. "You look starving, my lovely, and cold. We should get you some food and a blanket." I wrap my arm around her shoulders. I look back at Jay who is smiling at me. He motions me to go so I walk Elenor back to Dean's house to get her some proper food and some nice warm clothes.

Daniel

I sit there by the fire thinking about the recent events that have happened today.

"You okay?" Jay sits in the chair on the opposite side of the table and pours himself a drink.

"No, not really."

He sighs. "I can't imagine what is going through your head right now but I have your back, no matter what."

I smile at him. "What do I do, Jay?"

He lets out a small laugh. "To be honest, I don't know, have never been in this situation and probably never will be."

I look at him and smile. "You never know, you might have kids one day."

He cracks up laughing. "No, I don't think so; I'm not a family man and I'm not interested in getting a partner."

I raise an eyebrow. "You?" He looks at me. "You're not interested in getting a partner – someone you can have sex with day in, day out?"

He laughs. "You may have found someone that satisfies you but not me; I have never been satisfied." Interesting. "I don't actually think I have ever experienced an orgasm."

I choke on my drink. "Really?"

He laughs. "Nope. I hope I do get to feel satisfied one day."

I laugh at him, then my dad walks in the room. "She wants to see you."

My smile fades and Jay looks at me. "You heard Valdameir.

I can't."

Jay rolls his eyes. "Daniel, get off your ass and go in there. She is a fully-grown woman, capable of making her own decisions." He is right.

"Fine." I put down my drink and walk to her room. I see several water nation soldiers outside her room.

"Please leave the door open, my lord." I nod, remembering what Gemma said about them being over-protective. I walk into her room and see her sat by the fire in her favourite big jumper. She turns her head and looks at me with her puffy red eyes; she has literally been crying for hours.

"Why didn't you tell me?"

She stares back into the fire. "I didn't think you would believe me and to be honest no one knew apart from me and the doctor until I told Valdameir and Galina."

I sigh. "Why didn't you tell me first?"

She starts to cry again. "I didn't know how or what to do. I have never been so scared and part of you already knew."

I look at her confused. One of the soldiers walks in. "Are you okay, my lady? Would you like a drink or anything?"

She nods. "A cup of tea please."

He nods. "My lord, may I get you anything?"

I smile. "Same, please."

He nods and leaves the room. "That's their way of checking up on me."

I laugh a little then take a seat next to her. "What do you mean I already knew?"

She looks into the fire. "You knew before I did. When you produced that dragon on the battle field you turned round to me, eyes bright red, your whole body covered in fire – I thought you were going to kill me." I hate being reminded of that. "I have been thinking about it. You knelt down next to me placed your hand on my stomach and looked at me, gave me a kiss on the forehead then went back to normal." I am starting to see what she means. I did feel attached to that area of her and still do. "You weren't just protecting me, you were protecting your babies too."

I place my hand on her stomach and she places her hand on top of mine. "What also bothers me is that it's twins." Now I am confused. "If there is one thing, I do know about the water nation, one parent has to be a twin to have them." She looks at me. "You're not a twin, which means I'm a twin."

I start to think about what she has said then smile at her. "Listen, one day, if you want, I can help you find that twin but for now let's focus on getting you through this pregnancy and birth alive."

The soldier brings in two cups of tea and a few cookies. "Thank you." He smiles at us and leaves the room again.

"I want to have this family with you, Gemma, and I want you. I want you by my side for the rest of my life." She smiles at me. I move in front of her and kneel down. I lift up her top and touch her stomach. "Daddy can't wait to meet you both."

She smiles and moves in for a kiss. "Can you hold me tonight?" I nod.

Jay comes flying through the door. "Oh sorry, did I ruin a moment?" He grins.

Gemma laughs. "As always. What's up?"

I stand up and look at him, concerned.

"First of all, happy birthday." I look at the time and notice it's two minutes past midnight. "Second of all, you need to see this."

I nod and Gemma takes my hand then stands up. "It's your birthday?"

I smile and nod. "And the best birthday present was finding out I am going to be a father." She smiles. I tuck her hair behind her ear and give her a kiss on the forehead. "I love you."

She looks up at me and gives me a kiss. "I love you too. I will be waiting for you."

I smile at her and make my way out the door. I follow Jay out into the gardens and see my entire army, some being treated by the doctors and some looking like they are having their first decent meal in weeks. Derek comes up the stairs. "My lord."

I smile at him. I knew I could trust him. "Thank you so much!" I give him a hug.

"By the way, happy birthday, my lord." I laugh at him as he smiles. "My lord, we had some assistance from someone, an old man with messy grey hair, striped shirt and posh trousers." I look at him, confused. "He wanted me to pass on a message; he wants to meet you alone in the forest."

My dad walks up next to me. "Daniel, that is too dangerous."

I sigh. "He saved my army, the least I can do is respect his wishes."

Gemma walks up next to me and takes my hand. "You have your army back."

I smile at her, move behind her and place both of my hands on her stomach. "Yep, I have my army, my girl, my dad, my uncles and my best friend." I turn her around and look at her. "Most of all, I have two babies on the way and, like I said, that was my favourite present."

She smiles at me. "Happy birthday, Daniel."

I bring her down the stairs to meet my army and she does amazingly. Watching her talk to the army feels amazing. I have definitely met my forever love. Off in the distance I can see a man like the soldier described. He looks at me and walks into the forest. I walk over to the forest and follow him inside.

The forest is beautiful filled with fireflies and animals of every kind; bunny rabbits, deer and little birds. It is everything you can imagine a cute little forest to be like. I walk into this little opening with a small lake the size of a large puddle, I would say, but the water is clear and shimmering. You can see all the fishes inside it.

"Like it?" I jump out of my skin and turn to see the old man.

"It's beautiful. Gemma would love this place."

He smiles. "You really do love her, don't you?"

I nod as he smiles at me. He has a very warm grandad-looking smile. "Do you know who I am, Daniel?" I shake my head, still admiring the scenery. "I'm Azar, the dragon spirt."

I pause and look at him in shock. "You don't really look like a dragon?"

He laughs. "Neither do you, but you still are." He has a point. "I understand you have a few questions you need answering?" How did he know?

"Is he really my father? Dan Val Gule?"

He nods. "Yes, he is. I know you will be in denial about that for a while but over time you will learn to accept it but his story is true."

I nod at least I know that is true. "Gemma said that I knew she was pregnant before she did. How did I know without knowing?"

He smiles. "Why do you think Vision is so over-protective of you? Your inner dragon knows these things. Dragons are so over-protective of their babies; they will do almost anything for them and they can always sense their blood nearby."

Now I'm confused. "So, it was my inner dragon that knew? Why didn't he tell me?"

He laughs. "He can't talk to you, Daniel. He is merely your power source. He is the one that will help you sense your offspring nearby." That sounds weird. "Your power, Daniel, is extraordinary and there is a reason for it." I await the answer. "You are a member of the Karne family."

The who? "Who the fuck are they?"

He laughs. "My family. I am your ancestor." I am in a bit of shock after that. "Daniel, I need you to understand that to control the power within you, you need to follow everything Vang Chi tells you. He had no one to teach him but he knows that you are a lot more powerful than your father, him and Richard combined."

I take a gulp. "I'm scared of it."

He nods. "I understand that and you always will be. Learn to use it when necessary." I nod. "I have also given you a birthday gift." I smile and gave him a little laugh "I have taken back the fire nation for you in honour of the Karne name." I look at him in shock. I could cry. "Use it wisely but bear in mind you have a family to look after now; you can't just leave them." I haven't thought about that. "Daniel, I know you love Gemma but your love for her has put me in a complicated situation." I look at him funny. "No, I do not approve of the union. I'm afraid I do have the same views as your father but I understand that you love her." I feel slightly saddened. "I refuse to take this happiness away from you after all the trauma you have been through." At least he gets it, I suppose. "My only worry is that it will get you killed."

I sigh. "My father is claiming that they aren't mine."

He grins. "Yes, he is, but like I have just told you, the dragon within you sensed his offspring." I laugh a little. "They are definitely yours, Daniel, but Dan Val Gule must figure that out for himself." I nod. "There are tough times ahead, Daniel; your past will catch up with you. I know that you know that." I feel a little scared but happy that I have the support I needed. "I must go now, Daniel." He smiles. "Happy Birthday, and I will see you soon."

I bow to him. "Thank You, Grandad."

He smiles and disappears. I turn and walk back to the water nation house.

Gemma

I see Daniel come out of the forest and look at him, confused. "Hey, where did you go?"

He smiles at me and gives me a kiss. "To speak to my ancestor." I look at him like he is bonkers. He laughs. "It's a long story. I will explain later but he took the fire nation back for me."

I look down. I feel gutted that he is going to leave now.

"Hey, look at me, I'm not going anywhere." I get a bit confused. He smiles and faces his army. "Good Morning! It feels so good to have all of you back by my side and as a bonus an amazing birthday present! So, drinks on me tonight!" They all cheer. "I have a few announcements to make." They all turn to look at him. Even my army is intrigued. Dan Val Gule, Vang Chi, Richard and Jay make their way to the front. "The fire nation has already been taken back by the army that you saw invading them." They all cheer. He smiles. "However, we will not be going back there."

They all mumble between themselves and Jay looks at him, shocked. "My lord, what do you mean? That is our home."

He smiles. "Yes it is, and always will be. I will be knocking down the general's house and creating more homes for you. It will be a place for all of you to live, for you to rest, for you to raise your families in peace." They all smile. "I, however, will be staying here to raise my family." He looks at me and holds out his hand. They all look at me, confused. "The water nation general is pregnant with my children; she is the love of my life."

I smile at him and tears start streaming down my face. "All we want is what is best for both nations. I want all of my army to be happy and raise their loved ones in peace, where they know it is safe." They all look at each other. "Any questions?"

Derek raises his hand. "We fought for you, my lord, risked our lives for you, and you do this to us?" Oh dear. "I couldn't think of a better general to serve."

Daniel smiles as they all bow to him, including Jay. "Get up, Jay." He shoots up and walks over to Daniel.

"I knew you could do it." He gives Daniel a hug then moves over to me. "You have also taken up the mantel very well, my lady."

I smile at him I walk over to the members of my army. "Obviously, as Daniel has very kindly announced, I am indeed pregnant with his babies. In order for this plan to work, I will need your support, because this is also your home, not just mine."

Dean steps forwards. "My lady, we fought by your side, we protected you–" he smiles "–we will also do the same for your children, fire manipulators or water manipulators. We are honoured to protect and serve you, my lady." He bows and the rest of the army cheers. They all walk over to the fire nation army to socialise and get to know them.

Daniel walks up to me, wraps his arm around me and kisses me on the head. I look at him. "You are my forever now." I kiss him on the lips and wrap my arms around his neck. "Are you allowed to have sex while you're pregnant?"

I laugh at him. "In our situation, probably not a good idea."

I finally have the love of my life wrapped in my arms. I feel complete again. It might not last long but it is one hundred percent worth it.

I turn to see a man, the same man that the soldiers described.

I give Daniel a kiss and walk over to him.

"Hello, my lady."

I take a gulp as I look at his eyes; they are red. "You saved the army, didn't you?"

He smiles as he watches Daniel talk to Jay. "Yes, I did." I stand next to him and watch as the armies celebrate. "You definitely live up to your family name, my lady." I look at him, confused. I touched his arm but he pulls away. "Please do not touch me, my lady."

I take a deep breath. "You know of my family?"

He nods and gives me a cheeky grin. "And as will you soon but not yet; you must focus on the babies." I nods "I do not agree with this union but I will not break it. Daniel is finally happy. Just don't break him."

I all of a sudden feel depressed. "Who are you?"

He laughs. "My name is Azar, the dragon spirt. I am Daniel's ancestor." My eyes widen as I touch my tummy. He looks down at my tummy. "They will be powerful and challenging. I hope you are prepared."

I feel a rush of anger as he walks away. "I love Daniel, nothing will change that."

He turns. "I know, my lady, and he loves you." He walks up to me and touches my cheek. "You're an innocent young girl, beautiful and talented."

I sigh. "Well, I wouldn't say I'm any of that but whatever you say."

He grins then kisses me on the forehead. "You are all of those. You doubt yourself too much. You are about to become a mum; you must use that power within you to stay strong." I smile slightly. "Goodbye, my lady, I am sure we will meet again."

I hold my tummy and wave goodbye.

Vang Chi comes up behind me. "How did it go?" I look at him, confused, but he just gives me his warm cheeky smile. "Relax, I know Azar showed his face."

I sigh and look down. "He doesn't approve of the union but he knows Daniel is happy so he's not going to break it."

Vang Chi sigh and takes my hands in his. "I'm afraid Azar is basically another Val Gule; his beliefs are limited." He wraps me in his arms. Part of me wishes that Vang Chi were my father-in-law but it is good enough that he is here for me.

"You believe me, right?"

He smiles and pulls away, keeping his hands on my shoulders. "I do indeed and I can't wait to meet them."

I smile. He's started to become another Valdameir. Daniel is lucky to have him.

"Everything okay, babe?" I turn to see Daniel.

I smile at him and wrap my arms around his neck. Valdameir comes up behind him and crosses his arms. "If anyone was going to fall for a fire manipulator it was you."

I laugh at him and hug Daniel. "Well, I was raised by one."

I ran up to him, jump into his arms and wrap my legs around his waist. "Are you and Galina going to be here when I give birth?"

He holds me tight. "Of course. I need to meet my grandbabies."

I laugh. I kiss him on the cheek. "I love you, Valdameir."

He smiles. "I love you too, darling, as does Galina."

I smile so hard it starts to hurt. I remain in his arms until I crave Daniel's again, which isn't too long. I don't care what Azar has said, I am happy so I am going to hold on to it.

Richard

I walk round, meeting different members of Daniel's army with Elijah. Val Gule is walking round with Daniel and Vang Chi is walking round with Vince. I spot Jay leaning on the balcony looking over the army. Elijah comes up next to me. "Why don't you go and talk to him?"

I give him a little laugh. "What if he does find his father one day?" Elijah cracks up laughing. "What?"

He wipes a tear from his face. "With the type of luck that poor boys got his father is probably a cunt." He has a point. I decide to go and see Jay.

I walk up the stone steps and stand next to him. "You okay?"

He takes a sip of his drink. "Yeah, I guess I am."

I lean up against the balcony next to him. "You don't look it."

He chuckles then downs his drink. "I guess I'm just having a moment." He stands up and walks inside. I decide to follow. He goes and sits down by the fire in the great hall.

"What's up, mate?" I sit on the sofa next to him.

"I don't know, I guess I just feel a little bit jealous."

I laugh a little. "Of what? Daniel?"

He nods then refills his glass. "Yeah, I mean, Daniel has everything now and I still have nothing." I really do feel sorry for him because he isn't wrong. "He has a father, two uncles, a girlfriend and now two kids on the way."

I look into the fire. "I have always been jealous of my

brothers." He looks at me, curious. "Well, both of them are married. Unfortunately, their wives are very much dead but I have always wanted that but the only woman I ever loved was killed." He continues to listen to my story. "Dan Val Gule was blessed with a son and I can't have children." I sigh. "Vang Chi was blessed with strength and knowledge and I wasn't really blessed with any sort of power." I decide I am going to tell him. "And most of all they both know what sex feels like."

He spits out his drink and looks at me, shocked. "You have never had sex?"

I shake my head, then look at him, saddened. "My father had my testicles surgically removed when I was a kid, that is what I was told anyway." His mouth is wide open. "I have always wanted a son of my own. I have always wanted to get married and I have always wanted to feel like a man, like part of the family but never did." I look at him. "I always felt excluded, different, like I was a mistake, you know?"

He smiles. "Nah, you're not, you're just like me. You're more damaged and don't really know who you are yet."

I smile and nod. "The only thing I was certain about was having Valayrion and Elijah by my side."

He cracks up laughing and I notice Vang Chi standing right next to me. "Just Valayrion and Elijah?" I gulp. "Not your big brother Vang Chi, no?" I am definitely in trouble. "Richard, you have struggled all your life." He gives a pissed-off laugh. "I get it, you feel alone; I was never there for you and Val Gule is unfortunately never going to change – he will always be a drama queen –" I raised my eyebrows and looked at him, "but I'm here now. You're not alone anymore."

I look at Jay who smile then back at him. "Does that mean you're staying?" He smiles. I stand up and give him a massive hug. "Do you realise how happy that makes me, to have my big brother back?"

He holds out his arm and motions Jay to join. Jay rolls his eyes and gets up. He joins the hug. "None of you are alone anymore." We both pull away and smile at each other.

"Jay, if you want help finding your parents one day, I'm more than happy to help you."

Jay smiles at me then takes my hand. "Nah, I have everything I need right here." I look at him, confused. "Even if I did find my father, I don't think I would be lucky enough to have a decent one, so I will choose one instead." He smiles.

Tears start to fill my eyes. I look at Vang-Chi. "Another nephew."

He smiles at me. "At least this one is less challenging."

I gave Jay a hug. "Fun fact for you." I pull away and give him a curious look. "When I was a kid, I said to Daniel I have always wanted to meet the Ripper."

I laugh. Vang Chi is in stitches. "The Ripper?"

I nod at him. "I was given that name, I didn't choose it, trust me." Vang Chi is crying at this point.

"I was hoping you would come and rip Charles apart and save me and Daniel."

I laugh. "Trust me, if I had known, I would have."

He laughs. I hug him once more. Vang Chi then wraps his arms around me and Jay. Everything is falling into place.

Phillip

He's pissed off. Very pissed off. I walk up the centre of the camp after we retreat from the fire nation house and walk into the large tent in the centre of the camp. "My lord." He is sat at his desk in the centre of the room. To my right is the bedroom which has a simple double bed in it and just a few drawers. Two women are lying in the bed making out and touching each other.

"Why are you here?"

I gulped. "Well, I lost the fire nation, my lord. Some weird army I have never seen before has taken it over."

He laughs. "Daniel would have won it back anyway; he is too strong for you." He whistles and both women come over to sit on his lap. "Aren't they just beautiful." He begins to touch one of them.

"Yes, my lord."

He smiles. "Nowhere near as beautiful as the water nation general of course; she has an amazing body. Daniel's a lucky man." He kisses them both on the neck. "Get out." They both grab their clothes and run out the tent. He smiles at me. "I can still remember the feeling of her breasts." He is definitely imagining the water nation general naked. "I must admit, Valdameir is a clever man."

Valdameir? What is he talking about? "Valdameir my lord?"

He nods. He places his feet on the desk and stares into space. "If you weren't going to face Daniel you would have faced Valdameir, just like Charles did."

I gulp, knowing that he is right. "If you knew that I would have faced either Daniel or Valdameir, why did I take the fire nation?"

He laughs. "For Charles, of course, but you failed. Killing Daniel was for my benefit so that I can have Jay."

I roll my eyes. "Jay is nothing special. He is good in the bedroom, that's about it, and Charles was obsessed with him."

He looks at me with those bright blue eyes. "Is it not obvious? And yes, Charles was obsessed with him but since Charles was defeated by Valdameir I want him back."

My eyes widen as I realise. "You sold him to Charles?"

He shakes his head. "He was a gift from me and my wife. Charles is a valuable ally and I intend on getting him back."

I give a little laugh. "You know I was one of the ones that had my way with him, right?"

He smiles. "Oh yes, I am aware. Do you not miss it?"

I nod slightly. I'm not going to lie, I do miss it slightly. "He is a very good-looking lad under the clothing, I will admit."

He laughs. "Takes after his mother. She was a very good-looking woman. I don't marry ugly women. Shame she's dead."

I let out a small grin. "However, my lord, we have a more pressing problem."

He sticks his dagger into the table and starts to draw a mini drawing of his wife. "What's that?"

I gulp. "The water nation general is indeed pregnant with twins."

He smiles and lets out a little laugh. "Now that just confirms my theory."

I look at him, confused. "My lord, she will never survive from what I have seen, Daniel is far too powerful."

He cracks up laughing. "Of course, she will. She is probably one of the most powerful water manipulators in the water nation."

I looked at him, confused. "One of? My lord, that is not possible. Like I have said before, she is female."

He gets up and gets himself a drink. "Ah, Phillip, dear, you and everyone else in this world underestimates the power a female holds in this world." I roll my eyes. "Think about what you have seen her do. Have you seen any other water manipulator do that?"

I shake my head then realisation hits me. He grins. "All this time Valdameir was raising her."

He grins. "Indeed, he was. Like I said, Valdameir is smart; he knows his allies. However, he chose the wrong side, you know that."

I gulp. "What do we do?"

He smiles. "I must inform him of our finding."

I get a little bit on the confused side. "Him?"

He walks up to me and smiles. "Clive Mackenzie." Oh shit.

Azar

I look down upon this conversation between these two strangers and become slightly concerned. Elijah comes up next to me looking saddened. He is a tall skinny bloke but still has a lot of muscle to him, dirty blonde hair bright blue eyes and fair skin. He may be small but he is very quick and talented. He is also one of my best friends. "I feel like I have failed, Azar."

I nod at him. "Yes, you have." His eyes widen as I say that. "As have I. But we have time to make up for it." He gulps. He has never had to do this before. "There is one thing that is absolutely essential; Kai cannot know of any conversations between me, you and Alezaki." He has never looked so terrified in is life. "I understand you are scared of Kai, you will be a fool not to be."

He nods and slowly starts to cry. He is more upset that he wasn't there for Jay all these years. "Azar, I need to know what I can do to help him."

I give a small laugh as I watch these people make love to one another. "He is going to need support, that is granted, but Jay is very much broken already." I look at Elijah. "You may have failed, Elijah, but even Kai knows you always make up for it."

I pause as I move over to look down upon Daniel and Gemma. He has his arms wrapped around her waist. He looks so happy; I can't take that away from him after all those years of abuse. I look over at Elijah, who is looking down at Jay smiling. I walk over to have a look at what he is watching.

Jay looks happy. He is having a laugh with Richard. As a bonus, Richard look happy. It has been a long time since Richard has had a smile on his face. "I wish his own father could do that." He continues to smile. "What are you going to do about Daniel and Gemma?"

I go back over to watch Daniel. "I'm happy for him, although it does mean I have to work with Kai because those babies are going to be powerful." He nods.

Suddenly the doors fly open. I roll my eyes as a young-looking man with short dark brown hair, lily-white skin, icy blue eyes and a large muscular figure enters. Next to him is this beautiful woman, with a slim curvy figure, rather large breasts which are wonderful to look at, the most gorgeous dark brown eyes with long luxurious brown hair.

"Hello Azar." It is Kai and his wife Alentha. He slowly approaches me as I stand there with my hands behind my back. He came right up close to me. "We have much to discuss." He gave me his usual cheeky grin. So, it begins.